DATE DUE

DEMCO 38-296

In Nueva York

Nicholasa Mohr

Arte Público Press
Houston
Texas
1993

PS 3563 .O36 I5 1993

Mohr, Nicholasa.

In Nueva York

Mohr, Nicholasa.
    In Nueva York.
    Originally published: New York: Dial Press, 1977.
    1. Lower East Side (New York, N. Y.)–Fiction. 2. New York (N. Y.)–Fiction.
I. Title.
PS3563.O3615 1987 813'.54 87-18745
ISBN 0-934770-78-6

Cover design by Mark Piñón

Printed in the United States of America

Arte Público Press
University of Houston
Houston, Texas 77204-2090

For my brother and good friend,

Vincent C. Golpe

There is a country stretched across the sky
strewn with the rainbow's superstitious carpets
and evening's vegetation:
that way I go—not without some fatigue,
treading grave loam, fresh from the spade,
dreaming among those doubtful greens.

PABLO NERUDA

Contents

In Nueva York

Old Mary

Old Mary stood outside on the stoop steps of her building and looked for a spot that was fairly clean. The hard gray stone steps were worn, stained, and cracked, but she found a clean place near the loose railing where the surface was still smooth. Bending over, she set down an old plastic carseat cushion and squatted until she felt her bottom resting on it. She put down a copy of the Spanish newspaper *El Diario* and a cardboard fan, and held on to her can of beer. Quickly she snapped the metal tab on the can, feeling the light spray of cold liquid on her nose and chin. She gulped down enough beer to soothe her parched throat; then Old Mary belched and sighed, satisfied.

She raised her hand to feel the letter tucked safely in her bosom. She almost didn't believe it was real. After all these years—a miracle! God had heard her and taken pity. Yes, she would not die without a change of luck! When she first read the name and return address on the letter, she thought her wits were leaving her for sure! Old Mary quietly thanked God, making the sign of the cross.

She sipped her beer and looked up and down the street. It was early afternoon. Kids were still in school and most people were working. Except for a few old people sunning themselves, and an occasional drunk slumped against the side of a wall, most of the stoop steps and tenement doorways were empty. Down by the corner of Houston Street four men sat around an old battered bridge table held up by two wooden crates. They were playing a game of dominoes, while several other men watched. Here and there faces looked out of open windows. One small child stood up on the sill against a window guard. He was shrieking and bouncing to the percussion of a fast tune playing on a radio. He swung a wooden ladle as if conducting an orchestra and playfully waved it at Old Mary. She smiled and waved back with her cardboard fan. It was shaped like a Ping-Pong paddle. She looked at the tropical seascape printed on it. A golden sky shone brightly over green palm trees and a clear blue ocean. Gentle waves traveled slowly to the shore of a white sandy beach fronted by a large gleaming white building with lots of windows and terraces. Printed in black letters were the words: PUERTO RICO SHERATON · CONDADO · SAN JUAN · PUERTO RICO · COMPLIMENTS OF: RODRIGUEZ PHARMACY · LA FARMACIA DEL HOGAR.

Almost forty years since she had seen Puerto Rico! Well, maybe it was meant to be this way. She swung the fan back and forth, circulating the hot air. Old Mary began to sweat and felt the letter sticking to her flesh. She reached into the pocket of her housedress and pulled out a handkerchief. Carefully she removed the letter and patted it dry, then she wiped the cleavage between her breasts and put the letter back. It was a hot October day. A spell of Indian summer had sent the mercury rising up to eighty-four degrees.

Old Mary half closed her eyes and began to drift off when she was startled by a noise. She jumped and looked toward the metal garbage cans set out at the curb in front of the building. A large orange alley cat was rummaging through an open sack of garbage that had split and spilled out onto the sidewalk. She picked up her newspaper ready to scare it away, but abruptly, in midair, she stopped. Without dropping the piece of chicken backbone clenched in its mouth, the orange cat stared at her and yowled threateningly. She put down her newspaper.

"Ah . . . go on and eat, you miserable thing." She noticed that it was quite old and covered with sores. It blinked and stared at her, emitting several long piercing yowls.

"Shut up! I ain't gonna bother you, not today. And do

you know why? Because today my luck's turned. I've been given a chance—oh, yes! So you're in luck too. You see? One good turn deserves another. What do you say, yes?"

Keeping its eyes on her, it began to eat hungrily.

"Go on! I ain't gonna do nothing to you. Besides, look at you. No use even bothering about you. You're a mess, filthy and you're half bald. Your ears are chewed off! Your eyes are running with some sort of disease; you're practically blind. Bah! What a sight you are. Look, you got half a tail left and your belly droops!" Old Mary adjusted her glasses and looked down at her own swollen legs. She shook her head and laughed, pointing a finger at the cat. "You bastard you. You're still lusting around and fighting. You know what you are? A survivor, that's what you are—like me. And we even look alike, two old carcasses. Hah!"

The cat stopped eating. It licked its jowls vigorously and stared at her silently.

"You don't know enough to die either, do you? You're like Old Mary. You ain't got no sense in your head. You wanna keep on going, eh? Well, go on then, I ain't gonna bother about you. You don't have to worry about Old Mary. It's life—you old son of a bitch—life you gotta worry about. It'll fix you good!"

Old Mary sipped her beer, ignoring the cat.

Soon the kids would be coming out of school. Paco and Ralphy were supposed to be working after school, but she was never sure. They could tell her anything; what

6

could she do? Let their father worry for a change. A lot he cared—still in bed sleeping off a drunken stupor. Well, she was sick of Ramón and the way he spent his wages on drink. She was sick of them all!

As soon as Sarita came home from school, she would go up with her and wait for Doña Teresa. She was impatient to share her good fortune with her friend.

Old Mary finished her beer and leaned forward to see the large clock in the window of the luncheonette next door. It was ten minutes of three.

Rudi walked out of the store and began to unroll the green awning, casting a shadow on the sidewalk. At the base of the awning in white letters were the words: RUDI'S LUNCHEONETTE · SANDWICHES · SODAS · COMIDAS CRIOLLAS.

"Hola, Rudi, how's it going?"

"Hola, Mary, getting a little sun? It got hot today. October, imagine? I gotta roll out this awning because the sun is coming in too strong through the window. My pastries are gonna spoil." Rudi walked over to the spilled garbage. "Mira . . . bendito! Will you look at that?" The orange cat was gone. "Me cago en diez. For Christ's sake! Look at all this garbage will you? Damn cats. It's bad enough they don't collect regular . . . tsk!" He kicked the spilled garbage up against the cans, shaking his head. "I better get back. They'll be coming in any minute from school and them kids all wanna be served at once."

Old Mary looked at the assortment of garbage piled up

high. Plastic bags were so full that some had burst open. Today with the heat and the putrid stink of rotting food, the air was especially foul. The flies buzzed loudly, gathering in swarms, thriving.

"Whew . . ." Old Mary sighed. "It don't stop, it never ends."

A laughing, screaming group of young people passed by and chased each other into Rudi's. She smiled after them. How nice to be young like that, to have such energy. She remembered the letter. Oh, God . . . maybe I still have a chance. She looked down the street toward the corner, eagerly waiting for Sarita.

Old Mary sat in the small spotless kitchen with Doña Teresa. It had been a slow difficult climb up four flights of steps, especially on such a hot muggy day. But it was worth it to be with her friend. Doña Teresa had sent Sarita to wash up and do chores, so now they could talk privately.

"Mary, Sarita told me you seem upset, and I think she's right. What is it?"

"I am upset, Doña Teresa, and I got good reason. But I got even better reason to rejoice today."

"You must tell me. What's happened?"

"Yes, of course, wait." Old Mary reached into her bosom and took out the letter. "This morning I received this, and my life changed." She looked at her friend for a long moment, then clasping her hands together, she braced herself. "You are my best friend, and what I'm gonna say, I swear by all that's holy to me . . . nobody else knows. It's been my secret for almost forty years. It's something I made myself forget—until today."

Doña Teresa nodded and waited.

"Before you read this letter, I wanna tell you who it is that sent it." Old Mary smoothed out the envelope, pulled out the letter, and stroked it gently. "Almost forty years ago in Puerto Rico I had a baby, a son, who I ain't seen since he was an infant. This letter is from him—from my son William."

"Oh, my!"

"Nobody knows about him. And after all this time, to receive this . . . it's like a miracle." Her voice broke. She pressed her handkerchief against her mouth and sobbed quietly for a few moments, swallowed, then wiped her eyes. Doña Teresa leaned over, covered Old Mary's hands with her own, and pressed them lightly. Then she sat back ready to listen some more.

When Mary was thirteen her father and stepmother could not afford to keep her at home any longer. There were eleven other children to feed and care for. Her father secured a position for her as a domestic worker with a wealthy family in a nearby town. From the age of thirteen until she was fifteen, she was happy there. They were good to her and treated her justly. But the master had one weakness he could not control, and that was his desire for women. In less than a year she found herself pregnant. When she told the master that she was with his child, he gave her some money and got her a position as a domestic with another family in a large town far from her home. She worked there up to the last day before she gave birth. With the money he had given her, she rented some rooms and hired a good midwife. It was a tough birth, but the midwife pulled her through.

Old Mary paused and smiled, remembering.

"That baby was an angel, I tell you." She spoke slowly and carefully as if she too were listening and was afraid of missing a word. "He looked exactly like our Lord Jesus as an infant. William had such beautiful hair, blond, very golden, like a sunrise, and eyes as blue as the morning sea. His skin was very white and soft, almost transparent, like clouds on a clear day. Because, you see, his father was a handsome man. Distinguished and white. Oh, yes . . . whiter even than me." Old Mary lifted her arm and touched her skin. Doña Teresa looked at her arm and nodded. Old Mary had a very white complexion with a pinkish tone. "He had blond hair just like the baby and was tall . . . yes, at least six feet! That was his son all right. I knew that if he had seen that baby, in an instant he would know that William was his."

"Did he ever see the child? Or contact you? This man?"

"No . . . no, he was married with a family and had a prominent position. That could not be."

"Oh, but that's terrible. He had a responsibility. You were almost a child yourself."

"But still, I was just a worker, a servant in his house."

"You were a minor . . . innocent!"

"But he couldn't help it, you see. It was a weakness. That's the way it is for some men. Besides, you won't believe it now to look at me, but then I had long chestnut-colored hair"—Old Mary smiled and winked at her friend —"and a figure as firm and ripe as a fruit . . . ready to be eaten."

"What nonsense!" Doña Teresa shouted. "He couldn't help himself . . . tsk. This man was a pig."

"It was his weakness, I tell you."

"Weakness? But, Dios mío, he took advantage! Honestly, Mary."

"Come on . . ." Old Mary sighed and smiled. "Don't be upset. You are cross with me, ain't you? I can tell. It's because I ain't angry at him, or bitter, eh? Well, maybe you're right. I should be. But," she said shrugging, "it was all so long ago, and besides, since that time I've known worse, you see, oh, yes, a lot worse than him."

Doña Teresa opened her mouth to protest, but instead remained silent.

Old Mary continued with her story. Soon after William's birth she went back to work and left the baby in the care of others. Most of her earnings were spent on rent and for baby William's upkeep. When her son was just a few months old, she made arrangements to place him with a family who owned a small farm in the country and boarded children. She left for San Juan and quickly found work in a large hotel. There she was able to save some money and she planned eventually to keep baby William with her. But at the hotel all the workers ever talked about was going to New York City. In Nueva York, they said, the wages were high and opportunities greater. Some workers received letters from relatives in New York who promised a fortune could be made there. Old Mary knew she had to go there. She felt that was where her future was. She saved enough and purchased a one-way ticket to New York, confident that once she was settled she could send for her son.

Old Mary paused. She looked at Doña Teresa and the two women remained silent for a long moment.

"And that was the end of the story." Old Mary shrugged and touched the letter lightly. "Until now, to-day, forty years later. What's happened in forty years that I can add to the story, eh? I had seven more kids— four of them still alive. All this in William's lifetime, and we don't know each other. There's Chela, my oldest, who has kids of her own. Then Federico, who lives across the country some place—God knows where he is half the time! Then I still got Paco and Ralphy at home with me. None of them know that they got a brother in Puerto Rico. Do you know that my own father, God rest his soul, he never knew? First I was ashamed and then I knew his troubles and I didn't wanna add to them." Old Mary held up the letter. "I know . . . you're thinking, why didn't she send for her son like she planned, right? Well, I got to New York all right, but I was only here a short while and had another baby.

And no man wants an extra burden, especially one that ain't his. So it went, I had another baby and soon found myself alone again, this time with two small kids. I stopped sending money for William because I didn't have none to send. And I stopped writing because I didn't have nothing to say. I made no fortune in New York City. But I tried my best. I want you to know that. But I found my share of misfortune . . . and you, as my best friend, know that too. My kids ain't bad kids. They help when they can or when they remember. Besides, they ain't got much themselves. But the way it goes in this country, people are scattered everyplace and everything is so far away. Everybody lives in a place where you gotta take a train or a car or even a plane. Otherwise you lose contact. And then, I still got my burden to carry with Ramón. He's got the sickness of drink. Bendito! We never see a penny of his pay. He drinks it all before he puts it in his pocket. It was him who taught me to drink, you know. Oh, yes, he did! Before him I didn't know what it was to take a drop of drink . . . I swear it!" Old Mary made the sign of the cross, kissing her thumb loudly. "Of course, I don't take nothing stronger than beer. That's my limit, beer." She grinned, "Well, I gotta have some pleasure left in life, eh?"

Doña Teresa shook her head and laughed.

Old Mary placed the letter down in front of Doña Teresa, pushing it close to her. "Go on, my friend, I want you to read, and see what kind of a son I got. Jesucristo and la Virgen María have taken pity on me. They forgave me and sent a messenger of mercy. Go on, read."

Old Mary stared and waited impatiently as her friend read the letter.

"After all these years . . ." Doña Teresa looked at Old Mary wide-eyed. "It's just amazing!"

"See? You are affected deeply too. I knew you would be."

"And what determination he has, to keep on looking and not give up."

"That's right . . . and even now, you read how he begins the letter, excusing himself in case the reader ain't his mother. I guess, after such a long time, he's afraid to hope."

"But this time, Mary, luck was with him; he found his mother."

"True. You know, it was only by chance this all happened. The couple he spoke to that he mentions in the letter? Well, I ain't seen them in years. But I know the husband from way back. You see, he knew me and Fellín, my first husband. All of us sailed to this country together. I never told him about William, but he heard all them fights me and Fellín had about bringing my baby here to live with us. At first, when Fellín left me, he and I sort of kept in touch. And later, we would run into one another from time to time. I met his wife a couple of times; she's a lovely person. They told me they planned to retire in Puerto Rico and caramba! They must have made it. Dios mío, it was all so long ago. Imagine then, they were just passing by and William spoke to them.

Oh, it was more than luck this time, Doña Teresa; it was fate—God's work. And this time my son gets a reply, eh? No more 'address unknown' or 'no such person lives here'!"

"And then what, Mary? What are your plans?"

"Plans? But Doña Teresa, don't you see? Didn't you read? He's coming here to be with me and make me happy. He's got his airfare and he's willing to work at anything. I was like that, you know. I worked in my life . . . like una mula! I never said no to honest work . . . not like today! No sir! Everybody's afraid to work today. These young kids out there ain't made of the same stuff as me and William. And then, after we save enough money, I know how to economize, believe me. I had to. Why, we can move out of here. Out of this place. God, sometimes I'm afraid the building's gonna cave in. Like the building that collapsed near the Bowery. Remember? That baby was killed right in his own crib! God rest his soul. Well, but we're gonna move out. You see, we can find a clean house in a good neighborhood on a street where they collect garbage, and where you can walk without stepping on them filthy drunken bums. Or be afraid of them dope users. Criminals that attack hard-working people. Yes, we can find another place, because you see, William is white like me . . . and so it'll be easy; they will rent to us. It will be all right. We can find some nice rooms. And mira! You know that you and Sarita and your son Julian are welcome. Yes, always; you are my best friend. You are the type of people I want to visit me.

I can be proud to greet you. So you see my good fortune, don't you? Ain't you happy for me?"

"But of course I am." Doña Teresa hesitated. "Mira, I think you should talk this over first with Ramón or Chela before you—"

"No. I won't! It ain't their business if I send for my son. Besides I made up my mind. Ramón ain't moving with us. I'm gonna be rid of him, once and for all! As for Chela, she only knows how to take from her mother; and her brother, Federico, he never bothers about me. I could die for all he cares and he won't know till the funeral is over. Nevermind. And Paco, he can stay with his father—he's cut from the same cloth, that boy! Won't work. Won't go to school. But with William here to protect me, then Ralphy will behave. Maybe I can still do something with Ralphy. It will change. It will have to change because I am gonna have my son here to protect me. Don't you see? Like you got your Julian. He looks out for you and Sarita. Well, I'm gonna have that too."

"Now, Mary, listen to me. All of this is well and good. But you don't know nothing about your son, and he is forty years old. After all, he is no youngster; he must have some ties or some past life in Puerto Rico. You should know about this."

"But you read his letter. He says he has no one. There is nobody but me!"

"That's right, but he must have a past life. Everybody does. Then why don't he mention a wife or marriage or something?"

"He could've been married for all we know and it didn't work out!"

"Then what about children? Mira, you don't know nothing about him. It's true he's your son, but why don't you find out a little more before you leap ahead into something. What harm is there in asking?"

"Find out what? That he wants to come here to be with his mother? He told me that! That he wants to work and make me happy? He told me that! Doña Teresa . . . after all these years, how can I refuse him? I was the one that walked out on him, remember? He was innocent!"

"But I know that. I don't mean you should refuse him. All I'm saying is you should try to know a little more about him. That's all. Like what he's done with his life till now, yes?"

"But he will tell me everything when I see him. This way we can talk. I don't write too good anyway. So it's better that he be here in person. This way we got our whole lives left to talk." Old Mary paused, sighing. She carefully placed the letter back in the envelope and tucked it in her bosom. "Anyway, I'm grateful he forgives me, even if nothing else good happens. Other children would stay bitter and hate their mother."

"Mary, now don't go getting depressed about what I said. Things are gonna work out for you, I'm sure."

"Yes, I'm sure too. I got a good feeling about this. You know, I never lost my faith in God. I always prayed for a change of luck. You seen all the novenas and sacrifices

I made to the sacred heart of Jesus and the Immaculate Conception. I had that feeling for quite a while now. At first, I thought it was gonna be the lottery. I never buy a ticket without offering my little prayer to them upstairs, eh? Then I also kept dreaming about this one number and I thought, that's it, I'm gonna hit la bolita! But never-mind, now that's not important no more. What matters is that William is gonna be here with me. Now, right now, in my late years, when I need something like this the most. You see, Doña Teresa, when you're old and sick . . . well, I get scared sometimes."

Doña Teresa stood and walked over to Old Mary, plac-ing her hands gently on her shoulders. "Bueno . . . you know that I am happy for you. And if I can help you in any way, you can let me know. But you have to promise me that you will tell Ramón and the rest of your family. It's only right, if for no other reason. Yes?"

"I will . . . I will. Thank you. I know that I can count on you always. You and your children will be the only ones I'm gonna miss in this building. But those chismosas, gossips and loudmouths—they spoil the build-ing. You know how people like that give a building a bad reputation. Mira, I don't want them to know my new address."

"Mary!" Doña Teresa laughed. "You haven't written to your son and you already moved. Why don't you wait for an answer before you pack, eh?"

"Oh, but I'm writing to him right away, today! He said all he needed was a little bit of time to get things in order. I'll write him and give him my blessings and then I'll tell all of them about William."

She stood up with effort. "I better get down and see who's home and start my supper. Ramón laid one on last night and didn't get up for work. They're gonna fire him from that job! Maybe he's up by now. O.K., then . . . God bless you and your children, Doña Teresa."

Old Mary started down the stairway slowly at first, gripping the banister with one hand and supporting herself against the wall with the other. After a few steps she let go of the wall and quickened her pace.

"I never lost faith," she murmured. "God's work, yes sir. . . . That's what this is all about."

For the next three weeks people on the block had talked about practically nothing else but the arrival of Old Mary's son from Puerto Rico. No one really knew the full story, so many people invented their own stories.

One person spread the rumor that he was not really her son, but a half brother, whose father was very rich. He was actually being sent here, this person said, because his father had died and left all his money to his only son, who was slightly feeble minded. Old Mary was his only living relative. That's why she had such grand plans, because she was coming into money not rightly hers. Others said that William had been given up for adoption by her as an infant and was now the son of a well-to-do family. Now that he was grown up, he was just naturally curious and wanted to see what his real mother looked like. Some sight he'd see, they said. Once he saw what he'd come for, they were sure he'd take the first flight back to Puerto Rico.

But most people just accepted the fact that Old Mary was going to be reunited with her son.

On a crisp sunny Saturday in November several people stood outside Rudi's chatting as Old Mary approached them. Everyone noticed how, lately, it seemed she walked straighter and with a proud turn to her head.

"Hola, Mary; today is the day, eh? You must be busy."

"Yes, por fin, finally, today is the day. I've done most of the work, but I got a lotta last-minute things to do yet. You know how that is. . . ."

"Who's picking him up at the airport?"

"Bueno, Ramón, Paco, and Ralphy went with Chela's husband Frank and the kids. Frank is using his car."

"Good, you got a car to bring him. This way he can get here comfortable."

"Oh, sure. Mira, what those cabs grab you for at Kennedy, to bring you to the city, is as much as the airfare!"

"You're right. My nephew got stuck with a fifteen dollar bill. Can you imagine, fifteen dollars! Ave Maria, you gotta be Rockefeller to afford that."

"Terrible! And you know what is such a disgrace? Is that many times it's one of our own kind that do it." Old Mary shook her head.

"That's right, in this country—you don't trust nobody. But anyway, it's nice your son got nice weather today. Better than getting here in the winter with snow."

"Yes, thank God for that. We all gotta be grateful for the little things."

Everyone nodded in agreement.

"Well, I have to get going. We're gonna give my son a royal welcome from the whole family."

"Good luck!"

"Much happiness with his arrival, Mary!"

They all called out to her as she waved and stepped lively up the stoop and into her apartment in the back of the building. She could smell the food even before she opened the door. Inside, large pots were steaming on the stove. She could hear the roast pork sizzling in the oven. Chela was busy wrapping the cold salad dishes and setting out paper plates.

"Chela, did you finish with the rice pudding?"

"It's already in the refrigerator. Where were you, Ma? It's late."

"I had to do some last-minute things, that's all." She held out a small paper sack. "I had to get some stockings to wear tonight."

"Well, you better get dressed, Ma. They are gonna be here soon and then all them people are coming later. You invited an army for tonight."

"And what about your brother Federico? Has he called or anything?"

"No, you know him. He probably moved again and never got the message. Stop worrying about him, will you?"

"A whole army can get here but not him! But you're

right, Chela, on this day I ain't gonna worry."

Old Mary took a quick shower, then went to her room to dress. Carefully she examined her face in the mirror. She brushed her hair and pinned it back as usual into a neat knot at the nape of her neck. It was completely gray and thinning. Her broad face looked tired. There were many tiny wrinkles around her eyes. With her fingertips she pulled at them, lightly smoothing out the skin, then watched them reappear when she let go. She pressed the tip of her nose. Well, it's not so red now that I cut down on my beer, she thought, smiling. Quickly she covered her mouth to hide several missing front teeth. She opened a bureau drawer and took out her Coty cosmetic set, a present from Federico about two Christmases ago. She hardly ever used it. Old Mary looked at all the different types of powders and eye makeup. Lipstick and soft powder were all she could manage. She didn't know what to do with the rest.

She dipped the puff into the powder box and began to apply it on her face generously. God, I'm old, she thought. Too old for my age; I'm only fifty-seven. That ain't so old today. I read in the paper about that dancer, what's her name? She used to be a big movie star back some years ago. Ginger Rogers, yeah, her—caramba, she's gotta be my age! And she's marrying some young guy. She looks so young . . . almost as young as Chela. How could that be, eh? They say them women get plastic surgery and all that, and that they put on a lotta makeup. It's gotta be more than that! They never worked like mules, like me, eh? Never went hungry and cleaned toilets for a living. That's for sure.

Old Mary finished putting on some lipstick. What's William gonna think when he sees me? What's he expecting? He ain't never really seen me. That's right! Old Mary laughed and shrugged. So he won't know the difference of what I looked like once. When we meet, we'll recognize each other, that's all.

She replaced her old housedress with a long-sleeved navy blue crepe dress, and her sandals with black suede wedgies. She opened her jewelry box and looked at all the old pieces of costume jewelry and earrings that she had collected here and there. She found a small pair of pearl earrings that Chela had given her and put them on. Then she took out her most prized possession—her gold-plated butterfly pin. She pinned it on the left side over her heart, then stood back from the mirror to admire the green, red, and white shiny stones that covered the butterfly's wings. Old Mary looked at herself satisfied; she was ready to meet William.

They were late and Old Mary was getting restless and impatient. Frank's car was a second-hand Pontiac and often broke down on the road. She waited outside on the stoop and sat on her plastic cushion, sipping a can of beer. It was her first beer today, and the effect of the alcohol made her feel less anxious. She had thrown her coat around her shoulders to protect herself against the chill in the air. It was beginning to get dark and colder.

The street was almost empty except for one or two persons coming in and out of Rudi's. A few bums covered by flattened cardboard cartons slept soundly against the side wall of a building near the corner. Traffic was slow, but whenever a car turned into the block, Old Mary leaned forward and squinted, trying to see if it was the one bringing William.

Finally she saw Frank's car turn the corner and stop right in front. Quickly Old Mary stood up. Her insides were pounding so loudly that she could hear her heart and her pulses beating. The blood seemed to rush to her face and she was afraid for a moment that it might explode.

"It's only high blood pressure," she murmured and held onto the railing.

Rudi and several customers came out of the luncheonette to get a better view. Frank got out of the car first and then Paco and Ramón. Ramón went around and opened the back door. Ralphy stepped out followed by a little boy of seven and a girl of nine. They all stood by the side of the car, waiting. Everyone watched as a large head emerged, covered with thick, curly blond hair that shimmered with golden highlights in the dusky light of the evening. The rest of the person had broad shoulders, very short thick arms and legs; he stood no taller than three feet eleven inches. He was neatly dressed in a navy blue suit, white shirt, and tie. He smiled and looked around him and then he saw her. With a swagger to his gait, he rushed up the steps and embraced Old Mary. His arms circled the lower part of her shoulders and his large head rested on her chest.

"Mama, it's you . . . it's you," he whispered.

Old Mary gripped the railing and tried to pull away, but the small man held her tightly. She trembled, controlling her feeling of panic.

"It's you. Mama, it's really you!" He began to sob softly.

Old Mary looked around her. Who is this? Where's William? What's going on? Everyone looked back at her silently. Some were pointing to William. She wanted someone to help her.

"Mother of God," one of the people standing with Rudi whispered, "he's a dwarf!"

"Mama . . . Mama? It's me, William." His arms still tightly wrapped around Old Mary, he turned his face up toward her. She looked down and recognized him. He looked very much like her and he had his father's complexion and exact hair color. She glanced once more at all the people looking at her. Some of Rudi's customers smiled and nodded.

Slowly she released the grip on the railing and put her arms around the small man. Then she turned and nodded back at the people near Rudi's.

"All right . . . it's O.K." She spoke very softly.

"Let's go on in, Ma," she heard Ralphy say.

"Let's go inside, Mary." Ramón took her by the arm and placed a hand on William's shoulder. "Come on . . ."

25

William let go of Old Mary and took her hand.

The children jumped up the steps and walked along-side Old Mary and William.

"Abuelita . . . Abuelita," they shouted. "We like William so much. He's so cute!"

"I'm taller than him, Abuelita!" the boy said.

"No, you are not!" said the little girl.

"Yes, I am too!" The little boy stood near William. "I'll show you, wait . . ."

Old Mary and her family disappeared inside the building.

Outside Rudi and his customers remained silent for a while. They looked at each other, shrugged, and shook their heads.

"Do you suppose she knew about him?"

"I don't think so."

"Poor old lady, as if she don't have enough problems." Rudi sighed, "Tsk, tsk."

"Well, even if she did know . . . what could she do about it? After all, it's still a person. He's human, like everybody else, eh?"

"That's right. But she don't need this burden, that's for sure. I wouldn't want it."

"Well, he looks healthy enough to me!" Rudi smiled. "Did you see them shoulders? That's a powerful little man. And, who knows? He might be company for Old Mary."

"He's all right, just a little short for his age, that's all!" They laughed loudly with relief.

"Listen, I think that condition comes from lack of vitamins."

"What are you talking about? That's hereditary."

"I read an article once that said it's caused by the mother having a bad shock when she's still pregnant . . ."

"It's lack of vitamins that causes that, I'm telling you."

As they started back inside the store arguing, a loud crashing noise sounded. They turned and saw that the old orange cat had knocked the lid off one of the metal garbage cans set by the curb.

"It's that goddamn cat at the garbage again . . . coño!" Rudi chased the cat, but it only moved a short distance, just out of range. "Get outta here, you son of a bitch!" Rudi yelled and sprang forward, extending a kick in its direction. The cat hissed and growled back but did not move.

"It's all right." Rudi waved to his customers. "Go on inside. I'll pick this shit up." They continued arguing as they entered the store.

"Nobody knows what causes that."

"It's hereditary, I tell you."

Annoyed, Rudi picked up the broken paper sack and shoved it into the garbage can, covering it as best he could with the old dented lid. Wiping his hands on his apron, he called out to the cat, "I'm gonna get you one day, cabrón, you bastard!" Rudi looked around and picked up an empty can of beer. He flung it at the cat and missed. The cat remained perfectly still. Rudi sighed and went back inside to tend to his customers.

The old cat waited a moment, then leaped up on the garbage can and with great effort pushed and pulled until it knocked off the lid again. Carefully and skillfully it searched around in the broken sack and found something to eat.

The cat ate its meal undisturbed, except for the moments when it turned away to watch the people entering the building. Most were dressed up for the party and carried presents of welcome for Old Mary's son.

I

Never Even Seen
My Father

"O.K. then, Lillian . . . you tell me, what kind of person is he? A pervert, right? He's gotta be one." Yolanda puffed on a cigarette waiting for an answer.

Lillian sat in the small booth facing Yolanda, trying earnestly to answer.

"Look, I think all he meant was it's more of a subconscious wish on your part. Not like you really wanted to do it."

"But he said it was something I wanted. Can you imagine? I wanted it! Like I never even thought of such a thing . . . never, I swear."

"Yeah, but that's it, maybe you don't know that. But deep down inside your head, you don't know what your mind is thinking. Right? Nobody does, like dreams— you can't control dreams. Right? That's what psychology is all about, you see . . . getting way back in there down in your mind!" Lillian put her hand on the nape of her own neck, then rubbed the back of her head. "And seeing what makes people tick . . . mentally. That's what the doctor is talking about."

"All right then, you talking about dreams, right? And getting inside your head? Well, what about somebody like Doña Digna over on Rivington Street? What about her? She gets into people's heads and explains their dreams too, right? Do you believe what she says? A lotta people do!"

"Wait, Yolanda; now you're talking about espiritismo. . . . That's something else! That's not science."

"But people believe in it and they say she cures them."

"That's not science! There's no proof. You are comparing the science of psychology, something that is altogether different, to espiritismo, where you got no proof. The psychiatrist interprets your dreams and your subconscious to cure you of your problems, based on facts."

"O.K., you talking about facts, so let's say that Doña Digna tells you there is a muerto, a dead person, a ghost that is causing your problems, right? Then she'll get in touch with this ghost, who could be an evil spirit. . . . Somehow, she's got the power to fix things and cure your problems. People believe in that, Lillian. And you know I'm saying it right too!"

"First of all, there have been many, many books written on the science of psychology, and a doctor can tell you what's wrong—"

"What about all the dream books they sell? I seen them all over and so do you."

"Yolanda, you know them books are no proof; they are not scientific. With the right books a doctor can tell you what is wrong and cure you and—"

"He ain't gonna cure me. Because he's a sicko . . . really. He's putting things in my head I never even thought of."

"What will you girls have?" Rudi called out from behind the counter. The luncheonette was quiet during the early evening. Except for another customer at the counter, the store was practically empty. In about an hour the place would be busy with night customers. Rudi sipped a cup of coffee, enjoying the break.

"Gimme a coffee and . . . you got a piece of coconut cream pie? Good, I'll take a piece. Go on, Lil, order what you want. It's my treat."

"No, I'll buy." Lillian stood up and looked over at the glass display case against the wall behind the counter. She examined the pies, cakes, and puddings inside. "Gimme a root beer and a flan."

"Hey, Lil, I'm treating. I called you, remember?"

"But, you gotta save your money now."

"Forget it. I insist, Lil, otherwise I'm gonna feel bad. O.K.?"

Lillian smiled and nodded.

"Listen, Yolanda, I'm really glad you called me."

"It's been a long time since we seen each other privately and talked, huh, Lil?"

They smiled somewhat shyly as they remembered what good friends they once were. Lillian and Yolanda had been classmates and friends through grammar school and most of junior high. Then they went separate ways. Lillian was a good student and liked school. She found that most of her friends were good students like herself. Yolanda had never been very interested in school, and as the work became more difficult for her, she found that friends outside in the street were easier to be with.

"But you know you was always my ace! I respect you because you're smart and you always knew the answers. Everybody knows how smart you are, Lil." Yolanda hesitated. Nervously she put a cigarette in her mouth, then offered one to Lillian. "Smoke?"

"I don't smoke. Thanks."

Yolanda lit her cigarette, then bit her lip apprehensively. "Like I was saying, I know how smart you are and . . . well, that's why I had to talk to you about this. I know you could help me figure this out. Part of being out on probation is that I gotta stay in therapy with this jive-turkey doctor. And look, I know there's something wrong with me. Maybe a lotta things are wrong with me. Or else I wouldn't of messed up so badly. But, what he's talking about, it's . . . it's not my problem. And I'm not admitting to something like that. No way."

"Look, Yolanda, you feel like that because you don't understand what he means. I'm gonna major in psychology when I graduate next June. So I'm into that. What the psychiatrist means is that it's a symbolic meaning, not a reality, you see? Just a symbol."

"What do you mean a symbol? What does—"

"Wait. For instance, something that stands for something but doesn't actually look like or mean that something. Like an idea or a suggestion of a concept . . . "

"Lil, I don't know what you're talking about."

"O.K. The psychiatrist says you have"—Lillian lowered her voice and leaned over toward Yolanda—"a desire to go to bed with your father and you hate your mother. But he don't mean that really."

"What the hell does he mean then?"

"Wait, let me explain. He means that you act out your guilt about this desire and you punish yourself by being self-destructive."

"That's a joke. What guilt? Lillian, you know me and my family since we was kids, right? You know I never even seen my father! All I know is that when I was a baby he split and left my mother with three kids, and that's it! So then I got a desire to go to bed with somebody I ain't even seen? Come on." Yolanda inhaled deeply and vigorously blew out the smoke. "And then, I wanna do this or that because I'm guilty. So that means I'm punishing myself. . . . Man, that's ridiculous!"

Rudi set down the orders. "Enjoy yourself, girls." He went over to the other booths, carefully wiping down each table and seat with a clean damp cloth.

"One good thing about this place, Rudi still keeps it spotless."

"That's right, and he keeps out the bums too. I can't stand when they come in here all drunk, moaning and smelling."

"You're right, Lil, phooey!" They both laughed. "But it's good to be back." Yolanda sighed and drank her coffee. "You know, I missed the old neighborhood even though I thought I never would. It's funny, but I did."

"It must of been rough on you."

"Well," Yolanda put out her cigarette and began to eat. "Actually I was in a bad way, you know? . . . Girl, really wasted. Drugs messed me up bad . . . so I was better off in a rehab center than outside like I was. And I could've been in worse places. Anyway, I gotta lotta catching up to do. I gotta take some tests now to see where I fit back into school. I quit when I was fifteen, remember? You told me not to. You said, Don't do it, stick it out, don't quit. You were right, Lil, you're smart, I always knew that."

Lillian and Yolanda ate in silence for a few moments.

"You see, Lil, I gotta figure this business out first because I know that the doctor is wrong, and I'm not gonna admit to anything like he's asking."

"That's only because you don't understand." Lillian sipped her root beer. "He's trying to help, Yolanda."

"Understand what? Go on, you're smart. Tell me how he's trying to help me. I'm gonna tell you something I wish I could tell him. But I know I'll make it worse on myself because he don't wanna know about it. And, that's that there's a lot going on out there he, and even you, don't know about! You might read about it or see it on T.V., but that don't mean you know anything about what it's like to be hustling, stealing, mugging in a dog-eat-dog world . . . that's right, for survival, baby, in a sewer! Why don't he ask that? Why don't he ask me about the world I'm trying to split from? All he gives me is some jive-talk about my sexual desire for somebody I ain't never seen or met really. In fact, if I think of it, somebody I got me no use for."

"O.K." Lillian ate her last spoonful of flan, then took a deep breath. "I'm gonna tell you something. I'm gonna tell you a story about a Greek myth. Just listen to me, Yolanda. I've got my reasons. Just listen." Lillian stopped and waited until she was positive Yolanda wouldn't argue. "You see, the doctor's theory is based on a myth that was used by Sigmund Freud. He was a very famous doctor, a psychiatrist from Vienna. Now, this myth tells the story of a king back in ancient Greece, his name was King Oedipus. When he was born, the prophets said that he would grow up and kill his father, marry his own mother, and have children with her. When his mother heard this, she decided to have the baby killed. So she gives it to a servant to kill. But he feels sorry for the baby and gives it to a nobleman in another town, far away. When this baby grows up, he meets a blind man who is really a prophet, you know, someone that can tell the future? So this here prophet tells him about what is going to happen. That he will kill his father, marry his mother, and have kids with her. He leaves his town and runs away from his adopted parents, thinking that he don't want to do this to them, not knowing of course that he's not really their kid. Well, on his travels, he meets a man on the highway; they get into a fight, and he kills this man. Guess what? This man he just killed happens to be his real father! Now . . . he goes into the town where this man lives and he takes his place, marries this man's wife. And who is she? His real mother! They have kids and the whole thing comes true after all."

"Hey, wait a second, isn't his mother a little too old to marry such a young dude?"

"Well . . . maybe, but not that old, and probably in the old days it didn't make too much difference."

"What happened to his kids?"

"Wait . . . there's more. Somebody tells him the truth about his wife, you know, that she's his mother and that he killed his father and all. Well, he gets so upset and guilty that he pokes out his own eyes and goes blind. Then his wife kills herself because she's also very guilty."

"And what about his kids? Do they die too?"

"No, he goes away to an island in exile, and his kids just go to live with him."

"Yugh! That's some story."

"Right! So, from this myth is the theory of the Oedipus Complex. See? That's what they call the subconscious desire for one's father or mother. The Oedipus Complex, for King Oedipus. Now, because you feel very guilty for this desire, you punish yourself. It's a theory for treatment. Sigmund Freud discovered it."

"The doctor never explained it to me that way."

"There, you see then?" Lillian smiled, satisfied.

"Look." Yolanda lit another cigarette. "I gotta ask you something. Is that a true story?"

"I don't really know. I don't think so . . . it's more like a myth. You know, from ancient Greece."

"Do you believe this story really happened then?"

"Well, that's not important, whether it's true or not."

"It is to me! Just answer me if you believe it?"

"Yolanda, I already told you, my major in college is going to be psychology, and I've done a lot of homework on this already. Believe me, these things are facts."

"How can it be a fact if it ain't true? Now you tell me."

"The truth is the guilt . . . that's the facts—guilt and punishment."

"O.K., Lillian, guilt about what? Something that's not a true story?"

"You don't wanna understand, Yolanda . . . you don't!"

"All right." Yolanda hesitated. She pushed away her empty coffee cup and half-finished piece of coconut cream pie and leaned forward, placing her arms on the table directly in front of Lillian. "I'll tell you a story that really happened. O.K.? Doña Digna did a cure for my mother once. My mother was suffering from migraine headaches so bad she couldn't work, sleep, or nothing. When she went to Doña Digna for help, she said the cause of these headaches was that an evil spirit was leading my mother's guardian angel away from her. Now, this evil spirit was actually my mother's dead mother. That's right! Because when she was alive she had promised the Virgin Mary a novena and a sacrifice for a favor that the Virgin done for her. Somehow, her mother, you know, my grandmother, never kept her promise. So the Virgin Mary was making her pay her dues by sending her out to take her own daughter's guardian angel. The headaches were being caused by the guardian angel, who didn't wanna leave my mother because that's where the angel belonged. All right, so then Doña Digna tells my mother to complete the novena and do the sacrifice, you know, like wearing no shoes for six months or walking up to the altar on your knees eighty times—something like that. This way, her mother, my grandmother, will get off her back and leave her guardian angel alone. In the meantime, Doña Digna says her prayers and does her thing . . . man, and guess what? After my mother does all of this and Doña Digna finishes, my mother's headaches are all gone. And she don't get them no more. All right?"

"All right what?"

"All right, do you believe that story? It's true, you know

. . . I mean it's true my mother's headaches went away. She got cured!"

"It's not the same thing, Yolanda."

"It's a cure, ain't it?"

"The headaches got cured because they were psychosomatic."

"What's that?"

"That's where you give yourself an illness for psychological reasons. The cause is psychosomatic, mental and not physical."

"She still had bad migraine headaches even if they were . . . psy—psychromatic! And they went away. She got cured after Doña Digna solved her problem."

"You know, Yolanda, you are not giving the doctor a chance to cure you. I can see that. He's a scientist and Doña Digna is a—a spiritualist; that has nothing to do with science. You just won't listen and accept facts."

"What facts? So far you ain't told me no facts and neither did he!"

"Guilt, for one thing. Yes, that's a fact. People who are guilty because of things they can't face punish themselves. That way they keep from being successful and have an excuse for not living up to their potential."

"Why should I punish myself for something I never even thought of? You tell me."

Rudi approached them. "Hey, you want something else? You two looking so serious, eh? Cheer up, you young and good looking. What more you girls want?"

"Have another soda, Lil . . . go on."

"It's O.K., no thanks, I'm fine."

"Go on, give her another root beer and me another coffee." She smiled at Rudi and winked.

"Mira, there you go, that's better. You don't wanna go around looking like you have to carry the world's problems around with you, do you?" He walked back behind the counter.

"Well?" Yolanda leaned back in her seat and waited.

"Look, Yolanda, it don't matter if the story is true or not! Don't you see that? You just refuse to understand that! The doctor is only trying to find out why you do the things you do and"—Lillian lowered her voice, avoiding Yolanda's eyes—"got messed up and went to a . . . a place to get rehabilitated."

"But I wanna know why I did them things too. It does matter to me. Hey, Lil, it matters a lot! But what's a story about the olden Greek days got to do with me and the streets out there? Look, maybe I started on drugs because of a lotta things that might be wrong with me. Right? First of all, drugs are out there, available for anybody who wants to get high. And being high is a ball. You must think I'm sick to say that. But it's true, I swear it! And at the beginning everybody out there is real willing to get you high. Junkies want company, believe me, I'm saying it right. When you're high, it's beautiful, because you got no worries, man. You feel fabulous, you ain't scared of nothing and nobody. Your problems are over because you don't see where you live and you don't see what you ain't got and what you look like, and you don't miss what you can't see. Everything's perfect. But then you need more and more shit to keep you going. You don't get high so easy no more. You got to hang on to that feeling and you chase it like mad . . . you're not about to lose it. And the chase is a nightmare. Where you gonna get the money? Because by this time your body can't live without drugs . . . and you need shit just to feel normal, nevermind being high. Just feeling normal and not dying becomes your problem. And, you know, like my mother ain't got a cent, right? I can't even steal from her if I wanted to. I'm not smart like you, right? School turns me off. So what's left? Stealing and hustling. All your friends are junkies. You know you never gonna earn enough at no factory or being a salesclerk to support your habit. Because by now, it's taking several hundred dollars a day. A day! That's right! So you steal and you turn a few tricks and then you get yourself a man for protection. A pimp, so you got more rights on the street. Then you got more troubles than you need, right? Because now you got more than one habit to support, right? And there you are, part of that whole life scene, and it's got nothing to do with wanting to sleep with my father, who I never even seen, or some olden Greek times!" Yolanda stopped. She realized that Lillian's face was flushed and her cheeks were beet red. "Lillian, I'm sorry. I offended you. Look I didn't mean it that way."

Lillian turned away and reached into her handbag for a tissue. She blew her nose.

Yolanda reached over and touched Lillian lightly.

"Please, Lil . . . it's . . . " A scowl crossed Lillian's face as she looked at Yolanda. Yolanda withdrew her hand. "I said I'm sorry if I offended you. I shouldn't of talked out of turn."

"I'm not offended. It's all right; don't be silly."

"You see, Lil, it's very important to me that you know something. During my worst days, even on the street . . . when I had to—to well, when it was real bad—and I done things I don't wanna remember, I never, never, I swear to you that in my whole life, I never wanted to go to bed with my father. In fact, I don't remember even any dream like that. Please—please. believe me. I ain't sick that way, not like that!"

"Yolanda, yes, of course, but you still don't understand, do you? What—"

"Lil, just answer me one thing. Do you believe me? What I just said. Do you? Just answer me if you believe me, that's all."

They looked at each other silently for a moment, then Lillian whispered, "Yes, I believe you."

"Good!" Yolanda sighed.

"Here you are, young ladies." Rudi set down the drinks. "You want something else?"

"That's it. Thanks, Rudi. I get the bill."

"Just pay me when you're going out!" The door opened. "Here they come." Rudi greeted his customers. "I got some delicious carne guisada con papitas tonight, just cooked fresh." He pushed his blue plate special before taking orders.

The luncheonette was beginning to fill up with customers. The counter was almost full and the three tiny booths were occupied. A young woman walked out of the back kitchen and began to work at the grill. She worked rapidly, trying to fill the orders almost as quickly as she got them.

"Who's she?"

"Oh, you don't know her. That's Lali, Rudi's new wife. He brought her back with him from Puerto Rico, less than a year ago, I think."

"She's so young!" Yolanda whistled softly. "How about that horny old goat!"

"Isn't that something? You know he went to P.R. to get a wife, don't you? Because he knew he's not gonna find nothing like that here, right? My mother says he works her to death. You know, they could use some more help here with the business he's got, but . . . " Lillian shrugged. "Poor Lali, she's a little jibarita, a hick, from the mountains, so I guess to her this is living."

The door opened and Rudi called out.

"Hey! Chiquitín, come on, bendito! You're late. Let's go!"

William hurried by. He smiled and greeted Lillian. His shoulders brushed past the edge of their table.

"Who the hell is that?" Yolanda looked astonished after William.

"Oh, that's right, you don't know him either. Well, he's Old Mary's son, from the building next door. You know, Old Mary?"

"Yeah. She's still hitting the beer, I bet. Really? He's her son?"

"He came from Puerto Rico a few months ago to live with his mother. His name is William, but everyone calls him Chiquitín . . . on account of, well, his size . . . you know, he's so tiny."

"I can see why, wow! He's a dwarf, ain't he?"

Lillian nodded.

"But he's really nice, you know, like anybody else. He works here at night, part-time, for Rudi."

"Far out! Weird." Yolanda shook her head. "How old is he?"

"I don't know, but he don't look all that young. He must be like around thirty."

"What does he do, I mean besides work?"

"I don't know too much about him. I see him around. My mother says that he's trying to learn English. Taking a course at the high school or something. He works with Ramón, Old Mary's husband. He helps out on the truck. They say he's very strong."

"Yeah, he's got some shoulders. Beautiful hair too. It's so golden. I wish I had hair that color."

"Me too."

William walked over to their table and began to stack the dirty dishes in a large plastic basin he carried. His blue workshirt fit snugly around his shoulders. The sleeves had been cut, and his well-developed biceps bulged out, exposing a large tattoo on his left arm, just above the elbow, and a smaller tattoo on his right forearm. The large tattoo showed a colorful butterfly and the word MOTHER inscribed in each wing. The smaller tattoo was a decal of the Puerto Rican flag with the words MI PATRIA printed boldly underneath.

"Acabaron? Finish?" he asked, smiling.

"Sure." Yolanda took a cigarette and held it out to William. "Smoke? Go on, take it."

"Later—después, after work—yo—me smoke." He put the cigarette in his shirt pocket. "Gracias, thank you." He smiled.

"Hey, it's O.K. You're welcome. Enjoy it." Yolanda smiled and nodded as she watched him clear away the dishes and carry the large basin back into the kitchen.

"I told you he's nice."

"Man, I think I got problems and then I look at him." She shivered slightly, as if shaking off a chill. "Anyway, he ain't afraid to smoke and stunt his growth!"

They laughed out loud.

"Shh . . . " Lillian said, unable to stop laughing. Yolanda would stop laughing and then look at Lillian and they would begin to giggle again. They remembered how they used to laugh this way in school. It was as if they had a private joke no one else knew about, and when they looked at each other, only they could know how funny it was. After a while they stopped laughing and were silent.

The luncheonette was bustling with customers. Rudi hurried in and out behind the counter, serving and working the cash register. He called the orders to Lali in

Spanish. She worked without interruption, as if she didn't hear him. The juke box played a loud rock ballad.

"I gotta split, Lillian. I got me a date tonight."

"Yolanda, where are you staying? At your mother's? You didn't tell me."

"Well, right now I am with my mother, but she's got more problems than me. Like it's still the same there, so I don't know how long I'm gonna stay. Besides, I'd rather be on my own. I'm looking for a place around here on the Lower East Side. You know, I'm used to it here and I got friends here. My probation officer is a pretty nice woman; she's trying to get me into a school-work program. This way I can make some bread. You know, under one of the antipoverty programs. And, like I told her, I been a poverty program all my life, right? So what else is new?"

Lillian laughed. "You're still the same Yolanda. Listen, come to see us, O.K.? You haven't been up to my house for a long time."

"Yeah, sure."

"I mean it. I know, you think my mother would mind, but you're wrong. She knows I'm seeing you tonight and it's cool. Honest. Besides, we're the same age, you know. I'm not a baby."

"I dig. Lil, thanks."

They stood up. Yolanda paid the bill.

"O.K., Yolanda, you take it easy?" Rudi handed her the change. "The fast life slowed you up, eh?"

"That's right, Rudi. I slowed up, and you"—Yolanda

gestured toward Lali—"started making double time."

"Bueno, I gotta do the best I can, eh? For an old guy, me defiendo! I'm holding my own."

"Take it easy, Rudi, you know what they say about old dogs learning new tricks!" Yolanda winked at him.

"Don't worry about this old dog!" Rudi laughed. "Ave María, Yolanda you still the same, eh? Mira, take care of yourself. It's good to see you back looking so good."

"It's good to be back."

"Take care . . . "

"I'm trying, Rudi. I'm doing my best."

Outside it was cold and windy.

Yolanda leaned over and put her arms around Lillian.

"You're still my ace, girl. Keep on being smart and stay in school." Abruptly she turned and walked by the old orange cat sitting at the curb near the garbage cans.

Yolanda stopped for an instant and chuckled.

"You still around, eh? You old mother . . . "

The old cat blinked as it watched her dart across the street.

Lillian looked after Yolanda until she disappeared around the corner, then she started back home. As she walked she had a desire to run after Yolanda, to tell her once more that she must listen to the doctor; it was for her own good! She stopped for a moment and looked back in Yolanda's direction. Traffic rolled by steadily on the avenue. The headlights on the cars created bright silhouettes and long shadows in the darkness as they slipped in and out of sight. Lillian reached the stoop steps of her building. She stopped once more, thinking that Yolanda might never call again. This is silly. She'll call, why not? After all, she called tonight, right? I tried to help. I told her how it was. But, yes, Lillian sighed, she already knew Yolanda wouldn't call her. Shrugging, she ran up the steps, feeling, for some reason, and she couldn't figure out why, an enormous sense of relief.

The
English Lesson

"Remember our assignment for today everybody! I'm so confident that you will all do exceptionally well!" Mrs. Susan Hamma smiled enthusiastically at her students. "Everyone is to get up and make a brief statement as to why he or she is taking this course in Basic English. You must state your name, where you originally came from, how long you have been here, and . . . uh . . . a little something about yourself, if you wish. Keep it brief, not too long; remember, there are twenty-eight of us. We have a full class, and everyone must have a chance." Mrs. Hamma waved a forefinger at her students. "This is, after all, a democracy, and we have a democratic class; fairness for all!"

Lali grinned and looked at William, who sat directly next to her. He winked and rolled his eyes toward Mrs. Hamma. This was the third class they had attended together. It had not been easy to persuade Rudi that Lali should learn better English.

"Why is it necessary, eh?" Rudi had protested. "She works here in the store with me. She don't have to talk to nobody. Besides, everybody that comes in speaks Spanish—practically everybody, anyway."

But once William had put the idea to Lali and explained how much easier things would be for her, she kept insisting until Rudi finally agreed. "Go on, you're both driving me nuts. But it can't interfere with business or work—I'm warning you!"

Adult Education offered Basic English, Tuesday evenings from 6:30 to 8:00, at a local public school. Night customers did not usually come into Rudi's Luncheonette until after eight. William and Lali promised that they would leave everything prepared and make up for any inconvenience by working harder and longer than usual, if necessary.

The class admitted twenty-eight students, and because there were only twenty-seven registered, Lali was allowed to take the course even after missing the first two classes. William had assured Mrs. Hamma that he would help Lali catch up; she was glad to have another student to make up the full registration.

Most of the students were Spanish speaking. The majority were American citizens—Puerto Ricans who had migrated to New York and spoke very little English. The rest were immigrants admitted to the United States as legal aliens. There were several Chinese, two Dominicans, one Sicilian, and one Pole.

Every Tuesday Mrs. Hamma traveled to the Lower East Side from Bayside, Queens, where she lived and was employed as a history teacher in the local junior high school. She was convinced that this small group of people desperately needed her services. Mrs. Hamma reiterated her feelings frequently to just about anyone who would listen. "Why, if these people can make it to class after working all day at those miserable, dreary, uninteresting, and often revolting jobs, well, the least I can do is be there to serve them, making every lesson count toward improving their conditions! My grandparents came here from Germany as poor immigrants, working their way up. I'm not one to forget a thing like that!"

By the time class started most of the students were quite tired. And after the lesson was over, many had to go on to part-time jobs, some even without time for supper. As a result there was always sluggishness and yawning among the students. This never discouraged Mrs. Hamma, whose drive and enthusiasm not only amused the class but often kept everyone awake.

"Now this is the moment we have all been preparing for." Mrs. Hamma stood up, nodded, and blinked knowingly at her students. "Five lessons, I think, are enough to prepare us for our oral statements. You may read from prepared notes, as I said before, but please try not to read every word. We want to hear you speak; conversation is what we're after. When someone asks you about yourself, you cannot take a piece of paper and start reading the answers, now can you? That would be foolish. So . . ."

Standing in front of her desk, she put her hands on her hips and spread her feet, giving the impression that she was going to demonstrate calisthenics.

"Shall we begin?"

Mrs. Hamma was a very tall, angular woman with large extremities. She was the tallest person in the room. Her eyes roamed from student to student until they met William's.

"Mr. Colón, will you please begin?"

Nervously William looked around him, hesitating.

"Come on now, we must get the ball rolling. All right now . . . did you hear what I said? Listen, 'getting the ball rolling' means getting started. Getting things going, such as—" Mrs. Hamma swiftly lifted her right hand over her head, making a fist, then swung her arm around like a pitcher and, with an underhand curve, forcefully threw an imaginary ball out at her students. Trying to maintain her balance, Mrs. Hamma hopped from one leg to the other. Startled, the students looked at one another. In spite of their efforts to restrain themselves, several people in back began to giggle. Lali and William looked away, avoiding each other's eyes and trying not to laugh out loud. With assured countenance, Mrs. Hamma continued.

"An idiom!" she exclaimed, pleased. "You have just seen me demonstrate the meaning of an idiom. Now I want everyone to jot down this information in his notebook." Going to the blackboard, Mrs. Hamma explained, "It's something which literally says one thing, but actually means another. Idiom . . . idiomatic." Quickly and obediently, everyone began to copy what she wrote. "Has everyone got it? O.K., let's GET THE BALL ROLLING, Mr. Colón!"

Uneasily William stood up; he was almost the same height standing as sitting. When speaking to others, especially in a new situation, he always preferred to sit alongside those listening; it gave him a sense of equality with other people. He looked around and cleared his throat; at least everyone else was sitting. Taking a deep breath, William felt better.

"My name is William Horacio Colón," he read from a prepared statement. "I have been here in New York City for five months. I coming from Puerto Rico. My town is located in the mountains in the central part of the island. The name of my town is Aibonito, which means in Spanish 'oh how pretty.' It is name like this because when the Spaniards first seen that place they was very impressed with the beauty of the section and—"

"Make it brief, Mr. Colón," Mrs. Hamma interrupted, "there are others, you know."

William looked at her, unable to continue.

"Go on, go on, Mr. Colón, please!"

"I am working here now living with my mother and family in Lower East Side of New York City," William spoke rapidly. "I study Basic English por que . . . because my ambition is to learn to speak and read English very good. To get a better job. Y—y también, to help my mother y familia." He shrugged. "Y do better, that's all."

"That's all? Why, that's wonderful! Wonderful! Didn't he do well class?" Mrs. Hamma bowed slightly toward William and applauded him. The students watched her and slowly each one began to imitate her. Pleased, Mrs. Hamma looked around her; all together they gave William a healthy round of applause.

Next, Mrs. Hamma turned to a Chinese man seated at the other side of the room.

"Mr. Fong, you may go next."

Mr. Fong stood up; he was a man in his late thirties, of medium height and slight build. Cautiously he looked at Mrs. Hamma, and waited.

"Go on, Mr. Fong. Get the ball rolling, remember?"

"All right. Get a ball rolling . . . is idiot!" Mr. Fong smiled.

"No, Mr. Fong, idio*mmmmmm*!" Mrs. Hamma hummed her *m*'s, shaking her head. "Not an— It's idiomatic!"

"What I said!" Mr. Fong responded with self-assurance, looking directly at Mrs. Hamma. "Get a ball rolling, idiomit."

54

"Never mind." She cleared her throat. "Just go on."

"I said O.K.?" Mr. Fong waited for an answer.

"Go on, please."

Mr. Fong sighed, "My name is Joseph Fong. I been here in this country United States New York City for most one year." He too read from a prepared statement. "I come from Hong Kong but original born in city of Canton, China. I working delivery food business and live with my brother and his family in Chinatown. I taking the course in Basic English to speak good and improve my position better in this country. Also to be eligible to become American citizen."

Mrs. Hamma selected each student who was to speak from a different part of the room, rather than in the more conventional orderly fashion of row by row, or front to back, or even alphabetical order. This way, she reasoned, no one will know who's next; it will be more spontaneous. Mrs. Hamma enjoyed catching the uncertain looks on the faces of her students. A feeling of control over the situation gave her a pleasing thrill, and she made the most of these moments by looking at several people more than once before making her final choice.

There were more men than women, and Mrs. Hamma called two or three men for each woman. It was her way of maintaining a balance. To her distress, most read from prepared notes, despite her efforts to discourage this. She would interrupt them when she felt they went on too long, then praise them when they finished. Each statement was followed by applause from everyone.

All had similar statements. They had migrated here in search of a better future, were living with relatives, and worked as unskilled laborers. With the exception of Lali, who was childless, every woman gave the ages and sex of her children; most men referred only to their "family." And, among the legal aliens, there was only one who did not want to become an American citizen, Diego Torres, a young man from the Dominican Republic, and he gave his reasons.

". . . and to improve my economic situation." Diego Torres hesitated, looking around the room. "But is one thing I no want, and is to become American citizen"—he pointed to an older man with a dark complexion, seated a few seats away—"like my fellow countryman over there!" The man shook his head disapprovingly at Diego Torres, trying to hide his annoyance. "I no give up my country, Santo Domingo, for nothing," he went on, "nothing in the whole world. O.K., man? I come here, pero I cannot help. I got no work at home. There, is political. The United States control most the industry which is sugar and tourismo. Y—you have to know somebody. I tell you, is political to get a job, man! You don't know nobody and you no work, eh? So I come here from necessity, pero this no my country—"

"Mr. Torres," Mrs. Hamma interrupted, "we must be brief, please, there are—"

"I no finish lady!" he snapped. "You wait a minute when I finish!"

There was complete silence as Diego Torres glared at

Susan Hamma. No one had ever spoken to her like that, and her confusion was greater than her embarrassment. Without speaking, she lowered her eyes and nodded.

"O.K., I prefer live feeling happy in my country, man. Even I don't got too much. I live simple but in my own country I be contento. Pero this is no possible in the situation of Santo Domingo now. Someday we gonna run our own country and be jobs for everybody. My reasons to be here is to make money, man, and go back home buy my house and property. I no be American citizen, no way. I'm Dominican and proud! That's it. That's all I got to say." Abruptly, Diego Torres sat down.

"All right." Mrs. Hamma had composed herself. "Very good; you can come here and state your views. That is what America is all about! We may not agree with you, but we defend your right to an opinion. And as long as you are in this classroom, Mr. Torres, you are in America. Now, everyone, let us give Mr. Torres the same courtesy as everyone else in this class." Mrs. Hamma applauded with a polite light clap, then turned to find the next speaker.

"Bullshit," whispered Diego Torres.

Practically everyone had spoken. Lali and the two European immigrants were the only ones left. Mrs. Hamma called upon Lali.

"My name is Rogelia Dolores Padillo. I come from Canovanas in Puerto Rico. Is a small village in the mountains near El Yunque Rain Forest. My family is still living there. I marry and live here with my husband working in his business of restaurant. Call Rudi's Lunch-eonette. I been here New York City Lower East Side since I marry, which is now about one year. I study Basic English to improve my vocabulario and learn more about here. This way I help my husband in his business and I do more also for myself, including to be able to read better in English. Thank you."

Aldo Fabrizi, the Sicilian, spoke next. He was a very short man, barely five feet tall. Usually he was self-conscious about his height, but William's presence relieved him of these feelings. Looking at William, he thought being short was no big thing; he was, after all, normal. He told the class that he was originally from Palermo, the capital of Sicily, and had gone to Milano, in the north of Italy, looking for work. After three years in Milano, he immigrated here six months ago and now lived with his sister. He had a good steady job, he said, working in a copper wire factory with his brother-in-law in Brooklyn. Aldo Fabrizi wanted to become an American citizen and spoke passionately about it, without reading from his notes.

"I be proud to be American citizen. I no come here find work live good and no have responsibility or no be grateful." He turned and looked threateningly at Diego Torres. "Hey? I tell you all one thing, I got my nephew right now fighting in Vietnam for this country!" Diego Torres stretched his hands over his head, yawning, folded his hands, and lowered his eyelids. "I wish I could be citizen to fight for this country. My whole family is citizens—

we all Americans and we love America!" His voice was quite loud. "That's how I feel."

"Very good," Mrs. Hamma called, distracting Aldo Fabrizi. "That was well stated. I'm sure you will not only become a citizen, but you will also be a credit to this country."

The last person to be called on was the Pole. He was always neatly dressed in a business suit, with a shirt and tie, and carried a briefcase. His manner was reserved but friendly.

"Good evening fellow students and Madame Teacher." He nodded politely to Mrs. Hamma. "My name is Stephan Paczkowski. I am originally from Poland about four months ago. My background is I was born in capital city of Poland, Warsaw. Being educated in capital and also graduating from the University with degree of professor of music with specialty in the history of music."

Stephan Paczkowski read from his notes carefully, articulating every word. "I was given appointment of professor of history of music at University of Krakow. I work there for ten years until about year and half ago. At this time the political situation in Poland was so that all Jewish people were requested by the government to leave Poland. My wife who also is being a professor of economics at University of Krakow is of Jewish parents. My wife was told she could not remain in position at University or remain over there. We made arrangements for my wife and daughter who is seven years of age and myself to come here with my wife's cousin who is to be helping us.

"Since four months I am working in large hospital as position of porter in maintenance department. The thing of it is, I wish to take Basic English to improve my knowledge of English language, and be able to return to my position of professor of history of music. Finally, I wish to become a citizen of United States. That is my reasons. I thank you all."

After Stephan Paczkowski sat down, there was a long awkward silence and everyone turned to look at Mrs. Hamma. Even after the confrontation with Diego Torres, she had applauded without hesitation. Now she seemed unable to move.

"Well," she said, almost breathless, "that's admirable! I'm sure, sir, that you will do very well . . . a person of your . . . like yourself, I mean . . . a professor, after all, it's really just admirable." Everyone was listening intently to what she said. "That was well done, class. Now, we have to get to next week's assignment." Mrs. Hamma realized that no one had applauded Stephan Paczkowski. With a slightly pained expression, she began to applaud. "Mustn't forget Mr. Paczkowski; everybody here must be treated equally. This is America!" The class joined her in a round of applause.

As Mrs. Hamma began to write the next week's assignment on the board, some students looked anxiously at their watches and others asked about the time. Then they all quickly copied the information into their notebooks. It was almost eight o'clock. Those who had to get to second jobs did not want to be late; some even hoped to have time for a bite to eat first. Others were just tired and wanted to get home.

Lali looked at William, sighing impatiently. They both hoped Mrs. Hamma would finish quickly. There would be hell to pay with Rudi if the night customers were already at the luncheonette.

"There, that's next week's work, which is very important, by the way. We will be looking at the history of New York City and the different ethnic groups that lived here as far back as the Dutch. I can't tell you how proud I am of the way you all spoke. All of you—I have no favorites, you know."

Mrs. Hamma was interrupted by the long, loud buzzing sound bringing the lesson to an end. Quickly everyone began to exit.

"Good night, see you all next Tuesday!" Mrs. Hamma called out. "By the way, if any of you here wants extra help, I have a few minutes this evening." Several people bolted past her, excusing themselves. In less than thirty seconds, Mrs. Hamma was standing in an empty classroom.

William and Lali hurried along, struggling against the cold, sharp March wind that whipped across Houston Street, stinging their faces and making their eyes tear.

In a few minutes they would be at Rudi's. So far, they had not been late once.

"You read very well—better than anybody in class. I

told you there was nothing to worry about. You caught up in no time."

"Go on. I was so nervous, honestly! But, I'm glad she left me for one of the last. If I had to go first, like you, I don't think I could open my mouth. You were so calm. You started the thing off very well."

"You go on now, I was nervous myself!" He laughed, pleased.

"Mira, Chiquitín," Lali giggled, "I didn't know your name was Horacio. William Horacio. Ave María, so imposing!"

"That's right, because you see, my mother was expecting a valiant warrior! Instead, well"—he threw up his hands—"no one warned me either. And what a name for a Chiquitín like me."

Lali smiled, saying nothing. At first she had been very aware of William's dwarfishness. Now it no longer mattered. It was only when she saw others reacting to him for the first time that she was once more momentarily struck with William's physical difference.

"We should really try to speak in English, Lali. It would be good practice for us."

"Dios mío . . . I feel so foolish, and my accent is terrible!"

"But look, we all have to start some place. Besides, what about the Americanos? When they speak Spanish, they sound pretty awful, but we accept it. You know I'm right. And that's how people get ahead, by not being afraid to try."

They walked in silence for a few moments. Since William had begun to work at Rudi's, Lali's life had become less lonely. Lali was shy by nature; making friends was difficult for her. She had grown up in the sheltered environment of a large family living in a tiny mountain village. She was considered quite plain. Until Rudi had asked her parents for permission to court her, she had only gone out with two local boys. She had accepted his marriage proposal expecting great changes in her life. But the age difference between her and Rudi, being in a strange country without friends or relatives, and the long hours of work at the luncheonette confined Lali to a way of life she could not have imagined. Every evening she found herself waiting for William to come in to work, looking forward to his presence.

Lali glanced over at him as they started across the wide busy street. His grip on her elbow was firm but gentle as he led her to the sidewalk.

"There you are, Miss Lali, please to watch your step!" he spoke in English.

His thick golden-blond hair was slightly mussed and fell softly, partially covering his forehead. His wide smile, white teeth and large shoulders made him appear quite handsome. Lali found herself staring at William. At that moment she wished he could be just like everybody else.

"Lali?" William asked, confused by her silent stare. "Is something wrong?"

"No." Quickly Lali turned her face. She felt herself

blushing. "I . . . I was just thinking how to answer in English, that's all."

"But that's it . . . don't think! What I mean is, don't go worrying about what to say. Just talk natural. Get used to simple phrases and the rest will come, you'll see."

"All right," Lali said, glad the strange feeling of involvement had passed, and William had taken no notice of it. "It's an interesting class, don't you think so? I mean—like that man, the professor. Bendito! Imagine, they had to leave because they were Jewish. What a terrible thing!"

"I don't believe he's Jewish; it's his wife who is Jewish. She was a professor too. But I guess they don't wanna be separated . . . and they have a child."

"Tsk, tsk, los pobres! But, can you imagine, then? A professor from a university doing the job of a porter? My goodness!" Lali sighed. "I never heard of such a thing!"

"But you gotta remember, it's like Mrs. Hamma said, this is America, right? So . . . everybody got a chance to clean toilets! Equality, didn't she say that?"

They both laughed loudly, stepping up their pace until they reached Rudi's Luncheonette.

The small luncheonette was almost empty. One customer sat at the counter.

"Just in time," Rudi called out. "Let's get going. People gonna be coming in hungry any minute. I was beginning to worry about you two!"

William ran in the back to change into his workshirt.

Lali slipped into her uniform and soon was busy at the grill.

"Well, did you learn anything tonight?" Rudi asked her.

"Yes."

"What?"

"I don't know," she answered, without interrupting her work. "We just talked a little bit in English."

"A little bit in English—about what?"

Lali busied herself, ignoring him. Rudi waited, then tried once more.

"You remember what you talked about?" He watched her as she moved, working quickly, not looking in his direction.

"No." Her response was barely audible.

Lately Rudi had begun to reflect on his decision to marry such a young woman. Especially a country girl like Lali, who was shy and timid. He had never had children with his first wife and wondered if he lacked the patience needed for the young. They had little in common and certainly seldom spoke about anything but the business. Certainly he could not fault her for being lazy; she was always working without being asked. People would accuse him in jest of overworking his young wife. He assured them there was no need, because she had the endurance of a country mule. After almost one year of marriage, he felt he hardly knew Lali or what he might do to please her.

William began to stack clean glasses behind the counter.

"Chiquitín! How about you and Lali having something to eat? We gotta few minutes yet. There's some fresh rice pudding."

"Later . . . I'll have mine a little later, thanks."

"Ask her if she wants some." Rudi whispered, gesturing toward Lali.

William moved close to Lali and spoke softly to her.

"She said no." William continued his work.

"Listen, Chiquitín, I already spoke to Raquel Martinez who lives next door. You know, she's got all them kids? In case you people are late, she can cover for you and Lali. She said it was O.K."

"Thanks, Rudi, I appreciate it. But we'll get back on time."

"She's good, you know. She helps me out during the day whenever I need extra help. Off the books, I give her a few bucks. But, mira, I cannot pay you and Raquel both. So if she comes in, you don't get paid. You know that then, O.K.?"

"Of course. Thanks, Rudi."

"Sure, well, it's a good thing after all. You and Lali improving yourselves. Not that she really needs it, you know. I provide for her. As I said, she's my wife, so she don't gotta worry. If she wants something, I'll buy it for her. I made it clear she didn't have to bother with none of that, but"—Rudi shrugged—"if that's what she wants, I'm not one to interfere."

The door opened. Several men walked in.

"Here they come, kids!"

Orders were taken and quickly filled. Customers came and went steadily until about eleven o'clock, when Rudi announced that it was closing time.

The weeks passed, then the months, and this evening, William and Lali sat with the other students listening to Mrs. Hamma as she taught the last lesson of the Basic English course.

"It's been fifteen long hard weeks for all of you. And I want you to know how proud I am of each and every one here."

William glanced at Lali; he knew she was upset. He felt it too, wishing that this was not the end of the course. It was the only time he and Lali had free to themselves together. Tuesday had become their evening.

Lali had been especially irritable that week, dreading this last session. For her, Tuesday meant leaving the world of Rudi, the luncheonette, that street, everything that she felt imprisoned her. She was accomplishing something all by herself, and without the help of the man she was dependent upon.

Mrs. Hamma finally felt that she had spent enough time assuring her students of her sincere appreciation.

"I hope some of you will stay and have a cup of coffee or tea, and cookies. There's plenty over there." She pointed to a side table where a large electric coffeepot filled with hot water was steaming. The table was set for instant coffee and tea, complete with several boxes of assorted cookies. "I do this every semester for my classes.

I think it's nice to have a little informal chat with one another; perhaps discuss our plans for the future and so on. But it must be in English! Especially those of you who are Spanish speaking. Just because you outnumber the rest of us, don't you think you can get away with it!" Mrs. Hamma lifted her forefinger threateningly but smiled. "Now, it's still early, so there's plenty of time left. Please turn in your books."

Some of the people said good-bye quickly and left, but the majority waited, helping themselves to coffee or tea and cookies. Small clusters formed as people began to chat with one another.

Diego Torres and Aldo Fabrizi were engaged in a friendly but heated debate on the merits of citizenship.

"Hey, you come here a minute, please," Aldo Fabrizi called out to William, who was standing with a few people by the table, helping himself to coffee. William walked over to the two men.

"What's the matter?"

"What do you think of your paisano. He don't wanna be citizen. I say—my opinion—he don't appreciate what he got in this country. This a great country! You the same like him, what do you think?"

"Mira, please tell him we no the same," Diego Torres said with exasperation. "You a citizen, pero not me. Este tipo no comprende, man!"

"Listen, yo comprendo . . . yo capito! I know what you say. He be born in Puerto Rico. But you see, we got the same thing. I be born in Sicily—that is another part

68

of the country, separate. But I still Italiano, capito?"

"Dios mío!" Diego Torres smacked his forehead with an open palm. "Mira"—he turned to William—"explain to him, por favor."

William swallowed a mouthful of cookies. "He's right. Puerto Rico is part of the United States. And Sicily is part of Italy. But not the Dominican Republic where he been born. There it is not the United States. I was born a citizen, do you see?"

"Sure!" Aldo Fabrizi nodded. "Capito. Hey, but you still no can vote, right?"

"Sure I can vote; I got all the rights. I am a citizen, just like anybody else," William assured him.

"You some lucky guy then. You got it made! You don't gotta worry like the rest of—"

"Bullshit," Diego Torres interrupted. "Why he got it made, man? He force to leave his country. Pendejo, you no capito nothing, man . . ."

As the two men continued to argue, William waited for the right moment to slip away and join Lali.

She was with some of the women, who were discussing how sincere and devoted Mrs. Hamma was.

"She's hardworking . . ."

"And she's good people . . ." an older woman agreed.

Mr. Fong joined them, and they spoke about the weather and how nice and warm the days were.

Slowly people began to leave, shaking hands with their fellow students and Mrs. Hamma, wishing each other luck.

Mrs. Hamma had been hoping to speak to Stephan Paczkowski privately this evening, but he was always with a group. Now he offered his hand.

"I thank you very much for your good teaching. It was a fine semester."

"Oh, do you think so? Oh, I'm so glad to hear you say that. You don't know how much it means. Especially coming from a person of your caliber. I am confident, yes, indeed, that you will soon be back to your profession, which, after all, is your true calling. If there is anything I can do, please . . ."

"Thank you, miss. This time I am registering in Hunter College, which is in Manhattan on Sixty-fifth Street in Lexington Avenue, with a course of English Literature for beginners." After a slight bow, he left.

"Good-bye." Mrs. Hamma sighed after him.

Lali, William, and several of the women picked up the paper cups and napkins and tossed them into the trash basket.

"Thank you so much, that's just fine. Luis the porter will do the rest. He takes care of these things. He's a lovely person and very helpful. Thank you."

William shook hands with Mrs. Hamma, then waited for Lali to say good-bye. They were the last ones to leave.

"Both of you have been such good students. What are your plans? I hope you will continue with your English."

"Next term we're taking another course," Lali said, looking at William.

"Yes," William responded, "it's more advance. Over at

the Washington Irving High School around Fourteenth Street."

"Wonderful." Mrs. Hamma hesitated. "May I ask you a question before you leave? It's only that I'm a little curious about something."

"Sure, of course." They both nodded.

"Are you two related? I mean, you are always together and yet have different last names, so I was just . . . wondering."

"Oh, we are just friends," Lali answered, blushing.

"I work over in the luncheonette at night, part-time."

"Of course." Mrs. Hamma looked at Lali. "Mrs. Padillo, your husband's place of business. My, that's wonderful, just wonderful! You are all just so ambitious. Very good . . ."

They exchanged farewells.

Outside, the warm June night was sprinkled with the sweetness of the new buds sprouting on the scrawny trees and hedges planted along the sidewalks and in the housing project grounds. A brisk breeze swept over the East River on to Houston Street, providing a freshness in the air.

This time they were early, and Lali and William strolled at a relaxed pace.

"Well," Lali shrugged, "that's that. It's over!"

"Only for a couple of months. In September we'll be taking a more advanced course at the high school."

"I'll probably forget everything I learned by then."

"Come on, Lali, the summer will be over before you

know it. Just you wait and see. Besides, we can practice so we don't forget what Mrs. Hamma taught us."

"Sure, what do you like to speak about?" Lali said in English.

William smiled, and clasping his hands, said, "I would like to say to you how wonderful you are, and how you gonna have the most fabulous future . . . after all, you so ambitious!"

When she realized he sounded just like Mrs. Hamma, Lali began to laugh.

"Are you"—Lali tried to keep from giggling, tried to pretend to speak in earnest—"sure there is some hope for me?"

"Oh, heavens, yes! You have shown such ability this" —William was beginning to lose control, laughing loudly —"semester!"

"But I want"—Lali was holding her sides with laughter—"some guarantee of this. I got to know."

"Please, Miss Lali." William was laughing so hard tears were coming to his eyes. "After . . . after all, you now a member in good standing . . . of the promised future!"

William and Lali broke into uncontrollable laughter, swaying and limping, oblivious to the scene they created for the people who stared and pointed at them as they continued on their way to Rudi's.

The Perfect Little Flower Girl

Raquel Martínez sat in the tiny living room listening sympathetically to her good friends and neighbors, Johnny Bermudez and Sebastian Randazzo. As Johnny spoke, Sebastian dried his eyes and blew his nose.

"That's the way it is! So we figured out this here plan, you know, because Sebastian can't manage all by himself, what with his asthma and everything." Johnny looked at Sebastian, who smiled weakly.

"You know I'll help Sebastian all I can. Like always, I'm here anytime you need anything; you know that," said Raquel.

"We know that"—Johnny leaned over, squeezing Raquel's hand—"and we appreciate it. But Sebastian's gotta have some kind of income. Once I'm gone, how's he gonna live? You know he can't work or nothing . . . between his sickness and his nerves and all."

"And I'm not going on welfare again," Sebastian interrupted. "You know I can't take it. All those nasty questions, forms to fill out, then the running around before you get a few lousy cents! Raquel knows what I mean. Right? She has to put up with it, but her situation is different; not like mine. I mean, they take pleasure in crucifying me, and this time I won't survive . . . I know it!"

"You ain't going on welfare! So stop it! Besides I ain't leaving tomorrow, and we got this thing all figured out already. Man, what are you beefing about?" Johnny hesitated, then he spoke in a softer tone, moving closer to Sebastian. "It's gonna be all right. Let's explain things to Raquel, like we said we was gonna do. Okay? All right, you calm down?"

Sebastian nodded.

"Mira, Johnny, I didn't even know you went down to the draft board or nothing; now you tell me you getting married. Ave María, why didn't you two let me know, eh?"

"At first me and Sebastian didn't want nobody to know because we didn't know our own selves what to do. But then we figured out a way to work it all out. You know,

now that I passed my physical and everything, we got six weeks before I gotta report in. And like I told you, I informed them already that I was getting married and that I would have more responsibilities of a wife to support. They said all I had to do was bring in proof of marriage, like a marriage certificate, and they would make all the arrangements. This way, my wife would get her check every month."

"Wait a minute, Johnny, you know this person you plan to marry? Can you trust her? Because once she gets the money, you never know if she's gonna give it to Sebastian, or keep it—"

"That's no problem. She can be trusted all right. She's an old friend of Sebastian's, and I know her since me and Sebastian been together. That's about two years, right, Sebastian?"

"Two years this month, Johnny. She's an old and close friend, Raquel. I went to college with her. Her name is Vivian. She's a social worker, and her friend Joanna is a little younger. She's an elementary school teacher. They've been together for about five years now."

"And besides, they're more older, around Sebastian's age, so they'll be responsible, you know? Also, they got their own money, so I don't think they're gonna rip me off. I mean they got good jobs and everything."

"They agree too then? It's definite, Johnny, you gonna get married?"

"Yeah. I'm gonna marry Vivian, because she's the one

that's Sebastian's real good friend. We're gonna have a church wedding on account of Sebastian's so religious. It's gonna be just the way he wants it—"

"You talk like it's something I want!" Sebastian stood up. "Johnny, you could have avoided this. All you had to do was mention us—that's right! They don't want gay soldiers in the United States Army! Isn't that right, Raquel? So it's not something I want, Johnny."

"Will you quit it? We been through this. I thought you was gonna stop this crap! I said I got my reasons for doing what I'm doing. My mind's made up. It's only for two years. I'll learn me a trade and probably get stationed right here in the States and be coming home every weekend."

"Do you believe what he's saying, Raquel?" Sebastian sat, shaking his head, and for a moment remained silent. "What trade? The only trade you are going to learn, Johnny, is to fight and kill people out there in Vietnam. Don't you see what's going on right in front of you, on television? Everyday we see people getting killed on the news! Who's killing and getting killed, Johnny? All the guys that were gonna learn a trade. Vietnam, that's where you are going, Johnny!"

"What about all them soldiers stationed here in the States?" Johnny tried to control his temper. "And so what if I go to Vietnam? I never been no place west of Hoboken, New Jersey—wait a minute, yeah. I was in Atlantic City once . . . "

"If you wanted to travel, you could have said so. I

wouldn't have stood in your way, Johnny." Sebastian's eyes filled with tears. "I know what a burden I am. You don't have to go to the army to get away!"

"I didn't join, remember? I was drafted, remember?"

"Basta!" Raquel interrupted, speaking firmly. "You two are not gonna fight now because it's not gonna solve nothing anyway. Don't go getting upset, Sebastian. If Johnny made up his mind, why you gonna get sick? Now, you say you got a plan? Well, then, we'll talk about this plan."

She was used to their arguments and, more often than not, was able to bring peace between them. Many times Sebastian would become jealous and accuse Johnny of having another lover. Johnny would react by losing his temper and accuse Sebastian of faking his illness. But in spite of the arguments and frequent outbursts, the threats and recriminations, both men were devoted to each other. Johnny had been only seventeen and Sebastian thirty-four when they had moved into the apartment next to Raquel's. At first she had thought they were brothers. They had similar coloring and were about the same height and build. Friendship between the two men and Raquel Martínez and her large family had been established almost immediately. They visited each other without invitation and relied on each other without hesitation.

Johnny worked at a dress factory in the garment center. When he was not feeling ill, Sebastian worked part-time as a haberdashery salesman. But most of his time was spent in their apartment, taking care of the household chores as best he could. Sebastian suffered from migraine headaches and asthma attacks. Raquel and her children were always there when Sebastian needed help. The two men responded when Raquel was in financial trouble, in any number of ways. They helped when she was short on the rent or electric bill. When Raquel's children needed something she could not provide, they helped; like the time Tuto needed a sweatshirt and shorts for gym, or last month when Nitza had to have money for a class trip to Washington, D.C.

Raquel ignored the gossip of some of the neighbors and their disapproval of her relationship with the two men. She knew, for example, that Doña Teresa, who lived two flights above, had publicly expressed her opinion in Rudi's Luncheonette.

"If I had young and impressionable sons, I would not allow such a relationship to exist. It's disgraceful."

Everyone had heard Doña Teresa, and the word was passed on to Raquel, who had smiled and responded, "She's only upset because I don't ask her permission first. Well, I'm not impressed with such airs. Her blessings or her disapproval are the same to me. I still need money to buy a token to ride the subway!"

But then Raquel ignored gossip of any kind. She managed to care for her home and six children on the meager amount of money she received from public assistance. To this, she added her wits and her talent as a good cook. Raquel used this skill to make ends meet. She cooked for private parties, weddings, birthdays, and christenings.

During the Christmas holidays she made and sold pasteles —delicate meat pies made from plantains and tropical root plants, especially popular at that time of year. Rudi occasionally hired her to work for him on catered orders, or when he needed a couple of hours of extra help at the luncheonette, and paid her off the books.

"Come on now," Raquel urged, "let's hear about the plans. Where you gonna get married—you said in the church?"

"Yes, Father Mangione is going to perform the ceremony at St. Michael of the Apostles. That's my church now . . . although"—Sebastian lowered his eyes—"I don't go to confession anymore. Still, I couldn't forgive myself if I—if Johnny didn't have a Catholic wedding. Besides, Vivian is Catholic too. It will be a very simple ceremony, without the usual fanfare, so it will be performed in the rectory."

"You know, I'm nervous about this whole thing, man! Like I ain't never been married before!" Johnny said.

All three laughed. Sebastian explained that what they needed was Raquel's help in planning the reception, which was going to be an informal buffet in their apartment.

"Do you think we could work out something with you and Rudi's, downstairs? I know he caters, but we don't have all that much to spend."

"Sure. Let me talk to him first, though. As for me, you know I'll prepare everything and I'm not gonna charge nothing for my labor."

"Oh, no, Raquel!" Sebastian protested. "We don't want that."

"Yeah," Johnny agreed, "like we know it's hard work and everything, man."

"No!" Raquel shook her head emphatically. "Nevermind. That's my wedding present for you. I cannot, and I'm not gonna charge you, and that's finished!"

"Thank you, Raquel. You're our best friend. Isn't she, Johnny—the best."

"Nevermind, none of that business. Now, tell me how many people are coming because maybe we don't need to use Rudi's at all. Maybe I can do it all here and next door in my house."

"All the kids are coming. I mean that's for sure, right, Johnny?"

"Ave María," Raquel said, pleased. "They gonna be so happy."

"One more thing." Sebastian hesitated. "We would like just one more thing from you, Raquel?"

"What is it?"

"Well, like I said, it's not going to be a big formal wedding or anything, but Johnny's wearing a suit and tie, and Vivian is going to wear a cocktail dress with a short veil . . . and, well, I was wondering if . . . Hilda could be our little flower girl?"

"Hilda?"

"Oh, yes, Raquel. I would love to have her as our little flower girl. She would look so adorable, and it would make it, you know, somehow complete. If it's O.K. with you, of course?"

Raquel thought a moment. "Well, you been so good to her, Sebastian. I know you try not to play favorites with my kids, but we all know she's the one you like the best. And the way you encourage Hilda with her singing. You know, she thinks she's gonna be a great singing star some day." She looked at Sebastian for a moment with uncertainty.

"Look, Raquel, it's all right if you say no. I understand —I might be asking too much. I know how you feel about us, and that's what's important. But, well, I also know people will talk and gossip."

"Listen, Sebastian. I know you want the best for my Hilda, and I know you are a good person. You are both two gentlemen, so it's all right. She can be the flower girl . . . if that's what you want."

"Thank you, Raquel, I'm very happy." Sebastian choked back tears. "Of course Hilda has to want to do it."

"That one? Ha! You know she's gonna be thrilled. She can get all dressed up and be the center of attention. You got no worry there. She's gonna bother you about this when she finds out, from now on. She's not shy, that one! All right then, that's settled." Raquel continued, "Now, we gotta figure out how many people gonna be here and what kind of food we gonna serve."

"Johnny's been trying to locate his sister, but she's not at the last address, right, Johnny?"

"Yeah, but I'm gonna get in touch with the last foster home she was at and see if they know where she went. It's been over a year I ain't seen her. I know for sure there are a couple of people from my work that I'm inviting, maybe even three. And, I would like to get in touch with the Carrións, who live in Brooklyn. They're like the best foster family I ever lived with—real good people."

"No one in my family's coming, Raquel. First of all, they would never come here from Bronxville, never! I mean, my sister and my aunt are afraid of getting mugged if they shop in Bloomingdale's on Fifty-ninth Street and Lexington Avenue! Imagine them coming to the Lower East Side? Please."

"Maybe you should ask your parents anyway, Sebastian, just for a friendly gesture. After all, they still your family."

"What for? I mean, what would be the point? They don't wanna see me. Maybe if I were the one getting married, then they would figure that I'm straight, and all would be forgiven. But they will never accept me or my way of life. Besides, I know them, and I know my father meant what he said . . . so I'll invite them all to my funeral!"

"Come on, don't be talking foolish."

"It's all right, Raquel, I don't care. I don't miss them either. And I've got my friends to invite. So, let's see. Oh, yes, and then there are Vivian's friends and Joanna's friends. We have to count them also."

As they planned the wedding, they became excited by the idea of a reception. In the two years that Sebastian and Johnny had lived together, they had rarely entertained. And then it was another couple or a few friends for dinner. Raquel was always cooking for other people's parties. This time, she and her family would be part of the celebration. They discussed decorations and possible favors for guests.

"Man, I liked them matches that got your name on them. You know what I mean? Sebastian, remember we got some at the wedding reception when one of my boss's sons got married?"

"You like them, Johnny? You know, we could even get pocket combs as favors. I've seen them."

"Hey, that sounds better even, just so long as it's got my name—Johnny Bermudez—cool, man! Don't that sound great?"

"Bueno, you better make up your mind, because them things gotta be ordered. And then you gotta send out invitations; this all takes time." Raquel continued to advise them, and they listened eagerly to what she had to say.

A loud knock sounded and the front door opened. A young girl about fifteen and a boy thirteen walked in.

"Mami, where was you? We went looking for you down at Rudi's."

"I told your little sisters I was here. Didn't you see Nitza and Hilda? Who's home? Where are the rest of you?"

"All I seen was Hilda. She was playing with Charlie

and Rene, and she didn't tell me nothing about where you was."

"Never mind, Anna. What do you want?" She turned to the boy. "You too, Tuto, what's the matter?"

"Nothing," he said. "I just wanted to know where you was."

"¡Ay, Dios mío!" Raquel stood up. "Listen, I better go back in and check my brood. I gotta keep an eye on them. Especially that Nitza, she's twelve going on twenty-one."

"The kids can stay if they want," Sebastian said.

"No, it's late already, and I gotta make sure everybody gets their snack and then goes right to bed. But look, you two, figure out how many people are coming to the reception. If you want to come over later when the kids are asleep, we can talk about the wedding and everything else. Maybe it's better I come here; anyway, we'll see."

"Who's getting married, Ma?" Tuto asked.

"Johnny is getting married."

"Wow, can they do that?" Tuto looked at Johnny and Sebastian wide-eyed. "I didn't know it was allowed!"

"What are you talking about, eh, Tuto?" Raquel asked sharply.

"Didn't you say they was getting married?"

Anna began to giggle. Tuto felt himself blushing.

"I didn't say them two was getting married! Ave María, I said Johnny was getting married."

"You not gonna be together no more?" Tuto looked at Johnny and Sebastian once again.

"Por Dios—" Raquel shouted. "Who are you to ask such questions? Muchacho! Didn't I show you manners?"

Tuto's face felt hot and flushed and was beginning to twitch with embarrassment.

"Don't be hard on him," Sebastian whispered to Raquel. "It's only natural he should be curious."

"I will explain to him later; he don't gotta be rude! He knows not to behave like this with grown-ups, where it's not his business." She turned to her son. "Metio! Nosey . . . get inside. I'll see you later. You too, Anna. Go on!"

Quickly the two young people left.

"Don't be cross with him, please, Raquel."

"I don't like what he did, Sebastian. They gotta learn manners. I'm not raising a bunch of brats. I will explain everything to them."

"You got good kids, Raquel. Man, I wish I had me a moms like you." Johnny smiled. "Wouldn't had me none of them problems."

"They are good kids . . . " Sebastian agreed.

"Thank you, I appreciate what you both say; but they gotta stay good, too, you know? Okay, don't forget now, figure out things a little more definite, and we go on from there."

Raquel Martínez entered her apartment with mixed emotions—a sense of eager joy and apprehension. She could not wait to tell her children they were invited to Johnny's wedding, but the circumstances and the marriage bothered her. Shrugging her shoulders, she murmured, "That's life, they are good people, and it's not wrong. They only doing what they gotta do."

"Mami, where was you? Tuto and Anna says Johnny is getting married; is that true?" Hilda waited for her mother to answer.

"That's true. We all invited, and Sebastian says if you like, you can be the little flower girl."

"Me? Really?" Hilda jumped up and down, "Oh, my —oh, Mami, I never been a flower girl before."

A boy of eight and a younger boy of seven came running in.

"Is there really gonna be a wedding and everything?" they asked.

"Yes, I'm gonna be a flower girl!" Hilda yelled. "And we are all invited! Right, Mami?"

"Shh . . . quiet; all this screaming you gonna wake up the neighborhood. Let's all go into the kitchen. Call Tuto and your sisters, and I'll tell you all about it."

Hilda stood in the rectory of St. Michael of the Apostles, alongside the maid of honor and the bride-to-be. That morning Raquel had brushed her long dark hair until the highlights sparkled, then tied the white silk ribbons round the top, letting them fall so that they framed her face. Hilda had admired herself in the mirror, delighted with the image she saw. Her dress was white with pale pink lace appliqués. She wore nylon pantyhose, white patent leather shoes with rhinestone buckles, and carried a small white basket filled with white carnations and lilies of the valley. Her brothers and sisters had exclaimed their praises loudly.

"Wow, Hilda, you look really cute," Nitza had said.

"Yeah," Rene agreed, "you look like you could be on television and everything, man!"

"She looks more beautiful than that!" Charlie said proudly. "Hilda could be a movie star even, right, Mami?"

It was a pleasant Sunday morning, late in the month of July, and people had been out on the streets, as Hilda, Johnny, and Sebastian walked to the church of St. Michael of the Apostles. Hilda remembered how pleased she had been when people noticed her.

They had all met in front of church, and after a brief meeting with Father Mangione, were ready and waiting for the ceremony to begin.

It was very quiet at the small and dimly lit altar at the rectory; except for the bridal party and the priest, no one else was present. Hilda felt her heart beating; this was way more exciting than when she had made her first Holy Communion. *This is way more grown up.* Hilda smiled to herself.

Father Mangione beckoned to the bridegroom and the bride-to-be, and they stood before him with heads bowed. He then signaled to Sebastian and Joanna, indicating where they were to stand. Smiling, he looked at Hilda and pointed to a place beside Joanna.

"You stand there," he said. "That's a good girl, my dear." Hilda promptly curtsied in response.

"We are gathered here in the presence of God to join together in holy matrimony Vivian Stallone and John Anthony Bermudez as one . . . "

Hilda looked at Sebastian, who bowed his head with eyes closed, concentrating on every word the priest spoke. Then she looked up at Joanna, whose face had a pleasant, calm expression. Joanna returned her glance. She smiled and winked with self-assurance at Hilda. Blushing, Hilda turned away and lowered her eyes.

She knew Johnny and Vivian were not really getting married, not like other people who lived together and had children. I wonder if she knows Mami told me, Hilda thought.

When Raquel had explained to her children that they were all friends helping out each other, Hilda had asked if the two women were like Johnny and Sebastian. Her mother had replied simply, "Yes, there's them people who care for each other that way."

Then Rene had asked if it was supposed to be a secret. "Tuto says ain't nobody supposed to know, right, Mami?"

Raquel had answered that it was not really a secret. "It's only that we shouldn't be talking about it to nobody, because some people don't think it's a normal thing, the way they are. And they would become upset about it." Hilda remembered her mother's response when she had asked her if it was not a normal thing. "Well, for me it's not normal, icaramba! And for a lot of people too. But for them it's a normal thing. They're happy. Besides, it's not other people's business what they do. Only God can make them decisions, Hilda, like what's a normal thing and what is not normal or natural—and we ain't God!"

" . . . for here in the house of God . . . before His eyes, you shall be united as one . . . for eternity! Never to be separated, either in mind, spirit, or body. Sharing responsibilities . . . "

Hilda felt uneasy. Maybe you can't hide nothing here in church, where God lives. She wondered if Father Mangione knew about Sebastian and Johnny, and Vivian and Joanna, and was warning everybody to watch out. Hilda examined the bridal party; Sebastian's eyes remained closed, and his expression was one of deep concentration and prayer. Vivian and Johnny were perfectly still, listening respectfully. Furtively, Hilda again glanced up at Joanna, who was staring straight ahead without any emotion. He don't know nothing, Hilda sighed, feeling calmer. Mami was right, it's probably only God's business and not Father Mangione's.

After the ceremony, the bride and groom kissed politely, then everyone shook hands and embraced.

At the photographer's shop, color photos were taken first of the entire bridal party, then the bride and groom, the bride and maid of honor together, and the bridegroom and the best man together. Finally Hilda shrieked with delight when color photos were taken of her posing all by herself.

When the bridal party arrived, Raquel and her children, as well as a few early guests, greeted them with fistfuls of rice and shouts of joy. The reception was being held at Sebastian's and Johnny's; Raquel's would be used to accommodate the overflow of guests.

Raquel had managed to do all the cooking for the reception in Sebastian's and Johnny's kitchen and her own. She had used Rudi's electric slicing machine for the turkey and ham. He had not charged for its use, nor for the loan of the large coffee urn.

"Tell the boys it's my present to them; after all, they're my customers too." Raquel had thanked Rudi by inviting him, Lali, and Chiquitín up for a drink later.

"The place looks fabulous, Sebastian," Vivian said. She turned and saw a large square sheet cake which had their four names inscribed on it. "Vivian, Joanna, Johnny, Sebastian," Vivian read out loud. "My goodness, you guys did it up right, didn't you!"

"Come over here, Viv . . . and you too, Joanna." Sebastian took both women over to Raquel. "I want you to meet the person responsible for practically everything you see here, and the person you've heard me talk so much about. She did all the cooking. The only thing she didn't do was bake the cake; that was store-bought, but that's about the only thing! And her kids—you already know Hilda—her kids are wonderful. They decorated and worked to make this whole thing possible! Raquel, meet Vivian Stallone, an old and dear friend of mine, and Joanna Marsh, another friend."

"Please to meet you." Raquel shook hands with both women. "Raquel Martínez . . . "

Sebastian reached out to grab Rene and Charlie as they passed by. "And here are two of her children . . . the youngest ones, Charlie and Rene. Meet some friends." Sebastian introduced the boys, who quickly ran off. "You'll meet the others as the day goes by."

People entered and Sebastian went to greet them.

"Mrs. Martínez—"

"Call me Raquel, miss."

"All right, Raquel; then I'm Joanna. I want to tell you that your daughter Hilda behaved beautifully, and she knows what to do. I know kids. You see, I teach elementary school—the third and fourth grades. And I'm with them all the time. I can tell the sharp ones, and Hilda is a sharp ten-year-old!"

"Sometimes too sharp!" Raquel laughed, pleased. "But she's a good girl. They all good kids, my children."

"You've done such a nice job here . . . Raquel." Vivian pointed to the decorations and the food that had been set out on a large table. "I'm so glad Sebastian has you to count on." She moved closer to Raquel. "Now that Johnny is leaving, it's going to be hard for him. I mean, I'm not always available, not living close by and all—"

"I know," Raquel answered. "You know him a long time, eh?"

"Oh, God, yes! Sebastian and I met in college. We went steady for two years . . . we were even engaged. Not officially, but we thought at one time that we'd marry . . . "

Vivian shook her head. "We go back a long time, all right!"

"Hold it, Mami. Say 'cheese!'" Anna held up a small Instamatic camera and snapped a picture. Replacing the flash cube, she held up the camera once more. "Okay, you all wanna pose together, all three ladies. Get close and say 'cheese.'" Quickly she snapped another picture.

Raquel introduced Anna, who ran off to take more pictures. Joanna excused herself, leaving to mingle with the other guests.

"As I was saying, Raquel, it's so good to know you're next door." Vivian spoke in a soft manner, but her voice had a querulous quality. "Till Johnny, you know, Sebastian had been having a very bad time of it. And except for us, he's quite alone. I mean, he doesn't see his family anymore, and he doesn't really have any close friends. Of course, now, with Johnny, he's calmed down. But there was a time that . . . well, for years I never knew when I'd get a phone call telling me about another attempted suicide. It got to be too much! I had to stop being available every time there was a crisis in his life. After all, I have a job to keep me busy, and I couldn't keep dragging Joanna into it. It wasn't her problem, and I have my responsibilities to her . . . "

"But now things are better for him."

"Yes, much better after Johnny. It turned out to be such a stable relationship. And when I think of the way those two met! Imagine? Sebastian being discharged from Creedmore State Hospital and Johnny being released on probation for drugs! And there they were, going to the same rehabilitation center." Vivian paused, and the two women looked at each other without speaking. "And here I am." Vivian's voice was just above a whisper.

"You are a good person, Vivian. You doing what you feel is right."

"Well"—Vivian shrugged—"what the heck, when I was twenty, I wanted to be a bride. I wanted to be Sebastian's bride. Sixteen years later, it's happened, in a way." Vivian smiled at Raquel.

"Listen, Vivian, let me tell you something. In this world, people gotta survive; believe me, if you don't learn to survive one way or another, you never gonna get a chance to live. Sebastian and Johnny, they are no exception."

"You're right, Raquel," Vivian said, feeling better. "And, I'm happy for them." A new group of people walked in and they called out to Vivian. "It was really good to talk to you. We have to do it again, more and soon."

Tuto's cassette player was sounding off a medley of Latin, soul, popular rock tunes, and ballads. People were drinking, eating, and greeting one another. Raquel realized they would soon be spilling over into her apartment.

"Oye, Raquel!" Johnny shouted. "Mira, I want you to meet some people and my sister." Johnny walked over to Raquel with his arms affectionately around the shoulders of a young woman about his age. They were accompanied by a middle-aged man and woman and a young boy of twelve. "I want you to meet my sister Gena. This here is the best, Raquel Martínez." The young woman's dark honey-brown complexion did not hide her strong resemblance to Johnny. "And these are Clara and Nestor Carrión, and their foster son Eddie."

"Your sister looks a lot like you, eh, Johnny? Only she's prettier, of course!"

"What do you mean prettier? Man, she's a fea, ugly!" Gena playfully punched her brother. "No, seriously, man, esta negrita is beautiful, not like me. I came out white, but homely!"

"I'm glad you still got your sense of humor, Johnny. But listen, son"—Nestor Carrión spoke with the benevolent authority of a father—"now you married, and you got real responsibilities. No more running and fooling around, eh? You going off to the army, and there you gotta grow up. There they make a man out of you. I know what I'm talking about. I spent four years in the infantry . . . you hear what I'm saying, Johnny?"

"Ave María, Papa," Clara Carrión said. "You gotta excuse my husband. He's still talking about the army days and World War Two . . . all about the ancient history. You remember, Johnny, how Papa be talking about the army and the war business?"

"I remember."

"What you mean ancient history? Then it was World War Two, and now it's Vietnam. The army is still the army, and war is still war—you get killed just the same! Listen to me, Johnny, you gotta shape up there, you know what I mean? See, Mama, he knows what I'm saying—"

"Better you remember nice things about us, Johnny, instead of talking about war and killing. You know, mi hijo, we always think of you as part of our family."

"I always remember only good things, Mama. I know you and Papa Nestor did right by me. I know I was a bad little dude too! Cutting classes and playing hooky; and I even took off a couple of times. But, still, them was the best days I had, at your house. Man, Raquel, I wanna say right here, for everybody to hear: these are buena gente . . . good people! They came here today all the way from Brooklyn and even brung my sister, so you know they gotta care."

"Mira, Johnny! What's happening, baby!" someone shouted, and Johnny excused himself, taking Gena with him.

"You know, we only had Johnny in our house for a year and a half, when he was just about the age of Eddie here. He needed a lot of attention, he gave us a hard time. But within a few months he settled down, and we realized he needed a lot of affection. So then we gave him like extra care, you know? He responded very well, and we became very attached to him. Right, Papa?"

"Oh, yeah," Nestor agreed, "he was doing good in school and in sports, but then they took him back from us. It was all the mother's fault; she made them kids crazy. I don't know why, because she said the father was dead, but she kept insisting she could care for them by herself. Then, every time, they end up in a children's center; then another foster home. Pretty soon, Johnny starts with the drugs, messing himself up."

"Did you have his sister Gena, too?" Raquel asked.

"No, she was with another family. But she used to come to visit Johnny, and sometimes she stayed for the weekend. But she had a hard time too—even worse than Johnny, because she's so dark. Placing her was more of a problem. You know, a lotta people cannot believe they are brother and sister. She must look like the father, because Johnny looks like the mother, very white."

"I hope he don't get sent overseas to Vietnam, where all that killing is going on," Clara sighed. "Bendito, I want him to have a chance at a happy life."

"Nevermind all that now, Mama. He just got married, and everything is gonna be all right for him. Look at the bride; she's a nice person . . . very educated. To tell the truth"—Nestor lowered his voice—"I was very surprised. I mean, I never expected Johnny to marry anybody like her—una Americana—and she's a bit older than him too."

"That don't matter today, Papa. Women can marry younger men now. It don't make no difference here. We are not back in Puerto Rico. Here is more modern. Don't you think so?" Clara looked at Raquel.

"I don't say it's bad, Mama," Nestor interrupted. "In fact, sometimes an older person maybe to look after Johnny is a good thing. You know what I mean? Making a home for him and everything. Why, look at the man he lives with—Sebastian, the best man. He's older too and seems nice and also very educated. You know," Nestor smiled broadly as he spoke, "I'm very proud of that boy. Johnny did all right for himself!"

"He did the best he could." Raquel nodded and gestured toward the food. "You folks have something to eat, there's plenty food. How about you, Eddie? You like some soda? Come and meet my son, he's your age!" Carefully Raquel searched among the crowd, then called out, "Tuto, Tuto, come over here!" Quickly Tuto was by his mother's side. "Mira, this here is Eddie; he's with Mr. and Mrs. Carrión. You give him some soda and show him around. Everybody enjoy themselves, I have to see to things. I been acting too much like a guest."

Raquel began to attend to the guests, who complimented her cooking.

"Hola, Raquel," Chiquitín greeted her. He and Lali were drinking some fruit punch. "Everything turned out beautiful!" he said.

"Thank you. Where's the boss?"

"You know Rudi is not gonna leave the luncheonette for one minute," Lali answered. "As soon as we finish, we'll go down, and maybe he'll come up for a while."

The music stopped and Sebastian picked up a spoon and banged loudly on a large glass bowl.

"Quiet . . . quiet everybody! Please!" he waited until he was sure everyone was listening. "Before we go on with the rest of the party, it's entertainment time! I have persuaded a very talented young lady to sing for us." The children began to laugh. "Shh . . . listen! We are lucky enough to have one of the best singers on the Lower East Side here with us right now! She is well known in these parts, but for those of you who don't know her"— Sebastian paused—"I want to introduce the one and only Hilda Martínez!"

Everyone clapped and whistled as Hilda came forward.

"All right, let's clear this area so that Hilda can sing her song."

"Oh, man!" Charlie shrieked. Rene began to giggle and spin around.

"Shh, shh . . . " Nitza looked annoyed at her little brothers. Turning to her older sister Anna, she said, "Make them stop." Anna reached out, pinched Rene, and looked severely at Charlie. In an instant they were quiet.

Hilda had a clear deep voice with perfect pitch, and today Sebastian had urged her to sing. She had promised a special song for him.

"This song"—Hilda looked around trying not to be nervous—"this song is all about friends, and it's dedicated to Sebastian Randazzo and his friend Johnny Bermudez . . . and everybody else. Oh, and yes, it's called 'You've Got a Friend.' It's my own special arrangement. I hope you like it."

"Hooray!"

"Let's hear it!"

Hilda closed her eyes and hummed a popular ballad. "Ummmm . . . ummmm mmmm, you've got a friend . . . mm . . . you've got a friend. Winter, spring, summer or fall, all you got to do is call, mmmm and I'll be there yes, I will . . . you've got a friend . . . "

Hilda sang clearly, embellishing the words with emotion, swaying as she sometimes closed and opened her eyes, or spread out her hands and clasped them as if in prayer. Everyone listened, totally captivated.

"People can be so cold . . . they'll hurt you and desert you . . . they'll take your soul if you let them—Ah, but don't you let them . . ."

Sebastian tried to keep from crying as he glanced from time to time at Johnny standing with his sister. Others were openly moved to tears, blowing their noses and wiping their eyes. Raquel watched her daughter with pride.

Hilda hit her last bar, holding the notes longer than usual. ". . . all you got to do is call . . . and I'll be there, yes I will . . . you got a friend. You got a friend . . . a friend!"

There was lots of cheering and applause as people congratulated Hilda and her family.

The cassette began to play pop tunes once more. A few of the kids danced, demonstrating the latest steps. The guests continued to eat, drink, and make small talk.

After several hours, the cake was cut; the presents were opened, and just before the party was about to end, everyone drank a final toast proposed by Johnny, Sebastian, Vivian, and Joanna to "the perfect little flower girl."

The Operation

Angie and Rick Matilla had moved into their small apartment in the rent-controlled tenement on the Lower East Side four years ago in order to save money. They planned, someday, to buy their own home out in the suburbs of Queens or Brooklyn. Rick held down a full-time job as an assistant production manager in a food-processing plant. At night he attended a community college where he was completing his course work toward an associate degree in marketing. They had decided not to have a larger family until they could give Jennie a better life, in a safer neighborhood. In the meantime they guarded her carefully, and it was only during this past summer that she had been allowed to play downstairs in the street by herself. And then, it was only in front of the building and for short periods at a time.

Summer was over and school had just re-opened. The days were still mild and it remained light outside until early evening. This afternoon, a day in early September, Angie had given her daughter Jennie permission to play outdoors.

Angie stopped preparing supper and glanced once more at the electric clock placed on the wall over the refrigerator. It read five thirty, and she began to seriously worry. Jennie was never this late—never. Angie went into the living room and dialed Sandy's number. That's where she must be, playing over at Sandy's, and she just forgot to tell me, that's all.

"Hello, Sandy? This is Mrs. Matilla, Jennie's mother. Is Jennie there? She's not! Did she go to your house today? This afternoon? No. Not at all? O.K. She's probably playing outside because it's still so light out and forgot the time. Wait . . . wait a minute, Sandy. Sandy, are you there? Listen, honey, if she should come up to your house, please tell her to get home right away; that her mother said so. O.K.? Thank you."

Grabbing her keys, Angie locked the front door and went down the narrow stairway and out into the street. It was suppertime; most people were indoors. There were no children about. Angie walked along the block, carefully searching for Jennie on both sides of the parked cars and in the doorways of the tenements. She reached the corner and looked out at the busy avenue. Trucks and cars sped by; as usual at this time of day traffic was heavy. Jennie wouldn't come this far; she knew better. Angie sighed, turning back. She approached a group of boys carrying baseball equipment. They were returning home from the schoolyard, commenting and laughing goodnaturedly at the game they had just lost.

"Man. What a beating we took. Coño, man, it was your fault, Lefty! You lost the ball—man, qué pendejo, you let it drop right out of your fuckin'—oops, excuse me . . ." A boy of about fourteen looked at Angie.

"It's O.K." Angie smiled. "Listen, I want to ask you boys something. You just came back from the schoolyard, right? Did you see a little girl around there? She's seven years old, wearing a pair of dark blue dungarees and a red sweater." The boys looked at each other and shrugged. "She has light brown hair cut very short."

"Was she alone?" one of the boys asked.

"I think so—but I'm not sure. She had a Spaulding ball, she might've been playing by herself."

"I ain't seen nobody like that in the schoolyard." The boy turned to his friends. "Right?" Everyone agreed.

"Wait a minute—" another boy said. "We seen some girls, remember? They was playing rope over by the other end of the schoolyard."

"Go on. The lady said she's seven, stupid. Them girls was way older, like twelve and thirteen. Ave María, man, bendito, Lefty, you don't know the difference between girls seven years old and thirteen! No wonder we lost the game! You out to lunch, friend." The boys began to laugh. "Sorry, lady, we ain't seen her."

"Thanks." Angie went back to her building, but before going in, decided to look inside Rudi's Luncheonette. The large clock in the window read ten past six.

The place was busy. Angie looked around, not really expecting to find Jennie.

"Angie, can I help you?" Rudi called over the counter.

"I'm looking for my little girl Jennie. Have you seen her? Did she come in here today?"

"No . . . I don't think so, I didn't see her. Wait a minute." Rudi turned to his wife, who was packing outgoing orders. "Lali, you seen Jennie? You know, Angie's kid. You know Jennie, right?"

Lali stopped working and walked over to Angie. "Of course I know Jennie! How are you, Angie? No . . . not today. I didn't see her come in. Is something wrong?"

"No, it's all right. She went out to play and isn't back yet. She's probably over a friend's house and forgot to tell me— It's O.K."

"Mira, Angie, if I see her, I tell her to go upstairs right away. No te apures, don't worry." Lali continued quickly, responding to the look of concern on Angie's face. "I keep an eye outside. If I see Jennie walking or playing, I make sure to send her home."

"Thanks a lot, Lali; I appreciate it."

Angie checked the street one more time.

"Jennie! Jennie!" she called out.

Maybe she's upstairs in the hallway waiting for me. That's it! Angie raced up the four flights of steps until she reached the floor. The hallway was empty. She looked up at the skylight on the top landing.

"Jennie . . . are you there? Jennie!" She went up the last flight of steps leading to the entrance out to the rooftop. She can't be up here. No way is she allowed on the roof. She knows that. But—maybe, she's waiting for me. While I was looking for her, she was looking for me! Angie pushed open the heavy metal door and stepped out onto the rooftop. It was still light and she could see clearly that there was no one in sight. Her eyes roamed over the empty rooftops, occasionally stopping at a pigeon coop. Off in the distance, she saw the silhouettes of two tiny figures leaning against the edge of a roof. For a moment, Angie wanted to call out to them. Then she realized that they were on another street and they could hardly see her, much less hear her.

Taking a deep breath, Angie swallowed, trying to control her frustration at the feeling of hopelessness that was beginning to choke her. A little calmer now, she went back down to her apartment.

Of course, she went to visit her other friend, Caroline. That's it! She's such good friends with Caroline Thomas. Angie found the phone number and dialed.

"Hello, Mrs. Thomas? This is Angie Matilla, Jennie's mother. I'm just fine. How are you? Good. Listen, I hope I'm not disturbing your supper? Good. I'm calling to see if my Jennie is there. No? Have you seen her today? You haven't? O.K. Well, it's just that she's never ever late when I give her a time to come home. You know what I mean? Like she's always home right on time. No . . . she came home from school all right. I always pick her up at three, after work. Yes, I get off at two. I work over at Mays department store on Fourteenth Street. Yes, that's right. I took that part-time job so I could be home for Jennie. Really, your cousin works there? Well, I'm not in that department. I'm in the stockroom. Is that right? Well, listen, like I was saying. I picked her up. No— you're right, you can't be too careful. I don't want her walking home alone. It's too many blocks and she has to cross Houston Street and everything. What? Yes, I've seen Caroline's brothers picking her up too. What? I know . . . The papers are full of that story. . . . What's that? Well, after she had her after-school snack, she asked to go out to play for a little while. It's still so light out, so I said yes. You know, she's cooped up in school all day, then here in the apartment, so I figured she could go out for a little while. But that was at four. Yes, I know it's only been a little over two hours, but I told her to be home before five. She knows how to tell time. Yes, she does have a way of checking. You see there's the luncheonette downstairs. Yes, Rudi's. And it has a big clock in the window. No—no, it's working all right. I was just downstairs looking for Jennie, and I checked it myself. I know you would tell me if she was going over to your house—yes. It's just that Jennie only has two really close girlfriends. Sandy García and Caroline.

Right. Sandy is a nice girl. Yes, I know it's still early. Sure. She'll probably turn up any minute out of breath telling me she's sorry she forgot the time. Would you? Thanks, I would appreciate it. Yes, that would be a big help. And tell your boys she's wearing dark blue dungarees and a red sweater. Sure I know, even though you're a few blocks away, sometimes kids wander off. Thank you very much, Mrs. Thomas. I will—I'll let you know—I won't worry. Good-bye."

Angie hung up the phone and caught sight of the newspaper on the coffee table. She felt slightly nauseated and closed her eyes. Where's Rick? He should be home by now. God—today is not his night to go straight to school, is it? She ran into the kitchen and checked the calendar. Thank God he's home tonight; Angie sighed with relief. She glanced at the clock. Six forty. Walking back into the living room Angie picked up the morning copy of the *Daily News*. When Rick comes home, he'll know what to do. Reluctantly, she turned to page three and re-read the feature story:

THIRD CHILD TO BE FOUND DEAD

Another missing child's battered and sexually abused body was finally located in a vacant lot along the South Street docks early this morning. The body of seven-year-old Nina Gomez, missing for five days, was found early this morning by officers William Harris and Patrick Jefferson. Nina, a resident of the Lower East side, was lured away, police believe, by an old man who offered her candy. Police traced the crime to the public school that Nina Gomez attended. From information given by several possible eyewitnesses, the alleged killer is described as a white male, with gray hair, over fifty years of age, medium height. . . .

Angie closed her eyes and hiccuped; a burning sensation choked her as she tried to clear her throat. Why did I let her go out? After reading this story, I must have been out of my mind—dear God! What should I do? Rick, where are you?

"Jennie!" Angie called and began to sob quietly.

She heard the front door open and jumped up. Rick walked in.

"What's the matter, Angie? You crying?"

"Rick—I did a terrible thing—God . . ." Angie controlled her sobs. "I let . . . Jennie go out to play. Now she's missing. She hasn't come home!"

"What?"

"Jennie's disappeared!"

It took a while before Rick managed to calm Angie.

"There's no sense in carrying on like this. It's not your fault, Angie, come on. Look, we're wasting time—Sweetheart, let me go out and look for her. She's probably playing somewheres."

"Rick, I looked, I looked all over . . . I told you. I'm so scared, the newspapers and everything. Rick, should we call the police?"

"First let me go out and I'll check in the building. Let me do that. You stay here just in case she comes home—or there's a call."

"Call? What call? From who? Telling us what?"

"Angie, please! Maybe Jennie's lost. She could've wandered off someplace and not know how to get home. She might tell somebody where she lives, give them our phone number. Please, stay put. I'll be right back."

Rick went to each and every apartment, trying not to let his mounting fear take over his sense of reason. When the last family said they had not seen Jennie, Rick decided there was only one thing to do—they had better call the police right away.

Two patrolmen arrived and began to question them. They asked for a photo of Jennie for the newspapers. Nothing to worry about, they assured Angie and Rick. It was just in case they couldn't find Jennie before tomorrow. They were also told that if they didn't mind, a detective would like to come over later in the evening to question them some more.

After the police left, Angie and Rick wondered if they should call their families to let them know, or wait. Perhaps Jennie might come home after all.

At four o'clock that afternoon, Jennie went downstairs to play. She bounced her small Spaulding ball against the stoop steps. Then she stopped and looked for someone to play with. She saw some grown-ups, and older kids, but no one she could play with. She glanced at the big clock in Rudi's window. Good; it's only ten minutes after four. I got a whole lotta time. Jennie began to walk down the block, bouncing her ball. It was warm and pleasant, and the sun brightened the street.

She heard yowling and hissing and stopped bouncing her ball. Two cats sat at a distance of about five feet, eyeing each other. Jennie recognized one of the cats. It was the old orange cat that was always hanging around Rudi's garbage cans. Her mother had forbidden her to pet or touch him. "You'll catch something. Look at him, he's all dirty and full of sores and disease!" It was the orange cat that was making most of the noise. The other cat was not yet full grown. It was gray, with black stripes and white markings on its paws and forehead. The young cat looked around nervously, not knowing whether to run or stay. It looked up at Jennie and meowed. Jennie realized that the orange cat was protecting a small torn sack full of chicken guts that lay a few inches away. She walked over to the gray cat. Meowing, it retreated a few steps, then ran around the corner across the street and over to the stoop of an old abandoned building. Jennie ran after the cat. It meowed at her and waited. She stroked the cat's forehead.

"Poor little kitty . . ." It blinked, purred, and rubbed up against her. "You're so nice. You wanna play ball? Here." She held the ball out to the cat. Eagerly the cat sniffed it as if it were food, then turned away disappointed, running up and through the partially opened doorway into the building. "Wait a minute, kitty-cat. Come. I'll get you some milk—wait! My mother will give me something for you . . ." Jennie ran up the steps and followed the cat inside. It stood on the top of the first landing and meowed at Jennie.

"I said to wait a minute. Look"—she searched in the side pockets of her dungarees—"I bet I can find something for you." The cat looked at Jennie with interest and started back down. Jennie pulled out some lint and an old empty bubblegum wrapper. She held it toward the cat. "Sorry." She shrugged. "I don't got anything with me." Quickly the cat ran back up to the landing and disappeared.

"Hey! Will you wait? I told you I'll get you something. Don't you believe me, kitty?" She ran up the steps. The cat meowed and poked its head through an opening in the banister. Jennie looked up and caught the reflection of the cat's eyes. "Wait, I said, and I'll take you home, kitty-cat." She ran up another three flights until she reached the top landing. Looking up, she saw that the skylight had a huge hole, where the glass had shattered. The bright sharpness of the light coming through almost blurred her vision. She shaded her eyes with her hands and saw the cat. It stood up against the door leading out onto the rooftop, looking apprehensively at Jennie. As she went to pick up the cat, it hissed and struck out with its paw, barely missing her.

"Don't be scared, kitty. I won't hurt you, I promise." The cat bared its teeth and hissed, its tail pushed up and hair standing on end.

"You wanna go out for a little walk. Wait—" Keeping

her distance Jennie leaned over and pushed open the door. The cat leaped out. "I told you I wasn't gonna hurt you," she called out, following.

Out on the rooftop, she looked about for the cat but couldn't find it. "Kitty . . . little kitty, where are you? Here, kitty-cat. Come back! Don't be scared."

Jennie walked over to the adjoining rooftop. It was connected by a cement wall divider about three feet high. She caught a glimpse of the cat darting along several rooftops in the distance. Quickly Jennie climbed over the divider, running in the cat's direction. She climbed over three dividers and had one more to go before she could reach the rooftop where she had seen the cat. When she came to the last divider, Jennie realized that the next rooftop was separated by a space, a narrow airshaft about four feet wide. She looked over the edge, down into the airshaft. Five floors below she saw the bottom, filled with garbage and debris, strewn from one end to the other. Jennie carefully looked around, trying to see how she could cross over. But there was just no way.

"Shucks." She sighed, convinced she could not climb over. "Wait, kitty . . . I'll go downstairs through this building; then I'll meet you—and I promise to get you some milk." She looked once again in the direction where the cat had disappeared. "It's probably in the street already."

"I don't think you're gonna catch your cat, little girl."

Jennie looked up and saw an old man smiling at her. Startled, she retreated a few steps.

"Did she run away? Your little cat—did she run away?"

"She's not my cat. I just found her before in the street."

"You like cats, do you?"

Jennie nodded.

"I like cats myself. Independent, they are. Yessir. That's what I like about them. Some people think they're ungrateful and stuck-up, but it ain't so. It's just that they got minds of their own, they do." He looked at Jennie and smiled. She stood perfectly still.

"I was gonna go after her through this building and give her some food. She was crying before because she's hungry." She pointed to the airshaft. "I can't get over this way. . ."

"But the cat could, right? Sure, she probably jumped over that like nothing." The old man walked over to the edge of the roof and looked down into the airshaft. "Some drop! Well, you don't wanna go trying to do that, now do you?"

"Oh, no!" Jennie shook her head. "That's why I was gonna go through there." She pointed at the roof-door entrance.

"Well now—but you shouldn't be going through this here building. You see, it ain't safe. None of these buildings are safe. Where did you come up from?"

"Over there"—Jennie pointed, not sure of the direction from which she had come—"I think."

"If you wanna come with me, I'll take you back down. But do you know where you live?"

"Yes."

"Once I get you out in the street, will you know where to go?"

Jennie nodded. "Come on then. . . ." She did not move. He smiled. "I won't hurt you little girl—Look." The old man searched in his pockets. "Here, would you like some candy? I got two left." He looked at the candy carefully for a moment. "One's cherry flavored and one's coffee. Which one you want?" Jennie did not answer. "Would you like the cherry one? Go on, take it. It's O.K."

Jennie held out her hand and the old man put a piece of cellophane-wrapped candy in her palm. Carefully he unwrapped his piece of candy and popped it in his mouth.

"I can't be all that bad if I'm sharing my supper with you, now can I?"

"This"—Jennie sucked on her candy—"this is your whole supper?"

"Yep." The old man nodded and smiled.

Jennie smiled back. She liked him. His hair was white, thinning slightly, and he was clean shaven except for a slight gray stubble on his chin. He was clean, not like the bums she saw on Houston Street and the Bowery. She remembered how awful they smelled.

"You see, cats ain't the only ones that get hungry. Humans do too! Since we're having supper together, we might as well get acquainted. My name's Nathaniel Abrahamsen. What's your name?"

"Jennifer Matilla."

"You can call me Captain Nate. Everybody calls me Captain Nate. Can I call you Jennie?"

"That's what everybody calls me, Jennie. Are you a real captain?"

"Yep. I'm a tugboat captain. I was tugboat captain for over twenty years. Mostly here, right off the New York docks. Do you know what a tugboat is?"

"A small boat?"

"Right, but what does it do?"

"I'm not sure. . . ."

"It's a small but powerful boat with a strong engine that pulls in big ships, ocean liners, freighters, warships . . . takes them right up to the docks. Couldn't run no port without your tugboats. That's right! You must've seen them right here on the East River. Yessir!"

"Mister . . . Captain Nate, do you live around here?"

"Not exactly. I lived here last night, in this here building. Just like the cat you was chasing. I live here and there, and anywhere I can. When you're down on your luck, you can't be too choosy."

"Are you down on your luck?"

"Yep. I just got out of the hospital. I had an operation. Yessir, a real big operation, too. Did you ever have an operation, Jennie?"

"No. I was supposed to get one when I was little, on my tonsils. But then I stopped getting colds and I didn't have to get one. Does it hurt a lot?"

"It hurts some. I mean, they put me to sleep of course. That's so when they cut you up, you don't feel nothing.

But afterward, well, when them stitches heal—it's something fierce."

"Are you all better now?"

"Well . . . it takes a long time for old people to heal up and get better. You know, young people cure right away, but not old folks."

"Oh." Jennie swallowed her candy. "That was good. Thank you."

"Sorry I ain't got dessert for you. Only one course this evening."

"That's O.K."

"Yessir. You know how many stitches I got? Forty-eight stitches right here." He pointed to his chest. "All around, clear across my back."

"Wow. . ."

"Would you like to see my operation, Jennie? I'll show it to you if you like." Jennie grimaced. "Don't worry, it's all healed up and they already took out the stitches. But there's a great big scar you could see. Doctors said it was a miracle I survived. Lung cancer is what it was, you know. From smoking two and three packs of cigarettes a day, that's what they said. Gosh . . . that's hard to believe. I knew so many guys that smoked just as much as me and never got nothing. They're still smoking. But me? I had to get this sickness. Well? Jennie, would you like to see my operation? It'll only take a minute?" He started unbuttoning his shirt, then stopped. "We better go inside the building, on account of I might catch a bad chill in my chest. I don't wanna go back to the hospital. O.K.?"

"All right. . ." Jennie followed the old man through the door and onto the roof landing. The sun was beginning to set and it was not as bright as before. The landing under the skylight was dim.

"Can you see all right, Jennie? Good." He removed his jacket and put it on the banister post, then he unbuttoned his shirt and lifted it up. "See . . . look here."

"I can't see nothing," Jennie said.

"That's cause you're not close enough . . . come closer." Jennie did not move. "I'm not gonna harm you. Come on, take a look, you'll see one heck of a scar!"

Jennie came close and squinted. She saw a bright thin reddish line made up of swollen skin tissue, dotted with tiny vertical scars. It started at about the middle of his chest and extended right around almost the full width of his back.

"Oooooo . . . ugh!" Jennie whispered.

"See? What did I tell you? It'll be some time before you see another scar like that one. Do you wanna feel it? It's all healed."

"No, thanks. . . It looks like a burn. Does it hurt a lot?"

"Naw—not really. More like a bad sore, you know. Of course, sleeping on this here hard ground don't help me none."

"Don't you got no place to go?"

"Nope"—he sighed and buttoned up his shirt—"no place to go."

"Do you got kids someplace?"

"Not that I know of. Then, of course, my being a sailor out at sea and all, one can never tell."

"Will you go back to sea on your boat and be a captain again?"

"I can't no more . . . I'm too old." He put on his jacket. "Even if I could, they took away my union card back in 1954, so it wouldn't be no use because I can't get no work unless I got my union card."

"Who took your union card away?"

"The United States government did—on account of something called politics, Jennie. At least that's what they called it."

"I know all about politics and voting. My parents told me."

"They did? Good for them. Well, there used to be a time if you belonged to a certain political party, you got into real trouble here in America."

"Mrs. Brodsky, my teacher, told me about it. That's like the Democracies and the Republicans. Like one of them, right?"

"No . . . not quite. This here was a different kind of party. Hey, you know something? You're pretty smart, ain't you? How old are you anyway?"

"Seven."

"Seven? By gosh. Look at that! You know how old Captain Nate is? Guess." Jennie shrugged. "I'm seventy! That's right. So you see, we got that in common. Seven and seventy! Only a couple years difference, right?" Jennie laughed. "Well, now, we better get going back outside. Your mother's gonna be worried, I bet. And it's getting dark."

Jennie followed the old man. "Be careful, Jennie, watch your step; it's dark, and sometimes these here steps are loose and broken. . . ."

"Did you travel all over the world on your boat?"

"No. I told you, tugs only travel on canals and rivers. But I used to sail on large ships all over the world. Yep, I've been just about everywhere there is. . . ."

"Did you go to Africa . . . and the North Pole?"

"Sure. I've been all over. You name it. I've been there."

They continued to talk until they got downstairs and out into the street. "Now where do you live, Jennie?"

Jennie looked around her. "Oh. I know where I am— I live that way there, around the corner and then around the other corner . . . I'll show you."

They walked up to the first corner, then turned the second corner.

"Here's my block, and way down there is my house—"

"O.K., Jennie." The old man stopped. "Now you get on home, so you don't give your mother no worry. Go on now—and don't go playing on roofs no more. You hear? You never know who you can meet and it might be dangerous."

"Good-bye . . ." Jennie smiled at him. "I like you."

"Well, thank you, Jennie, and I like you too. When you see the tugboats over on the East River, you can think of Captain Nate. Good-bye. . . ."

Realizing it was nighttime, Jennie rushed toward her

building. She reached the luncheonette and looked at the large clock.

"Oh, it's a quarter to eight," she murmured, racing up the four flights of steps. As she approached her door, she hesitated, afraid to face her parents. What should I say? Jennie felt her heart pounding. She thought about what she had done and realized that everything, going out of the block, chasing the cat, the roof, even talking to Captain Nate, everything was wrong. Maybe I can sneak in. She turned the handle very carefully. I hope it's not locked. The door opened. Good, she sighed. She heard her mother's voice on the telephone. With great care she closed the door and stood against the wall of the tiny foyer, wondering how she could get past her mother and into her bedroom.

"I know, Delia. It's still early, but it's very dark out now. No. Don't tell Mami yet. You know how bad her nerves are. We're just gonna wait for a couple of hours more . . . maybe she'll turn up by herself. God . . . I'm praying. What? Yes, we gave them her picture, you know, the small class photo they take each year. . . ." Angie lifted her head and saw Jennie's shadow across the threshold of the living room. Blinking, she caught her breath. ". . . What? Nothing, nothing is wrong. It's O.K. Listen, let me call you back, Delia. I said I'm O.K. I'll call you back! Good-bye."

Angie replaced the receiver and coughed before speaking.

"Jennie! Jennie! Come in here!" Very slowly Jennie

walked in, her eyes wide open as she saw her mother's rage.

"Where were you?" she yelled. "For God's sake—where were you?" Jennie burst into tears. "Stop it!" Angie yelled and rushed over, grabbing Jennie by the shoulders, forcefully shaking her. "Do you know what we've been through? Do you? Do you know what me and Daddy have gone through?" Jennie began to sob loudly. She looked at Angie, terrified.

Rick and Angie seldom yelled at Jennie, and except for one or two spankings when she was very little, Jennie had never been roughly treated.

Angie looked into Jennie's frightened eyes and stopped shaking her. "Oh, my God. What am I doing to you?" Putting her arms around Jennie, she stroked her back gently. "I'm sorry, angel. I'm sorry. It's just that Mommy was so scared . . ." Jennie's sobs lessened as Angie held her very still for a while, kissing her hair and her forehead. "O.K., darling?" Jennie nodded. "Let Mommy wash your face with a warm washcloth. . . ." Angie started toward the bathroom and abruptly stopped. "Oh, what about Rick? Jennie, Daddy is outside right now looking for you and he's very worried . . . what should I do? I'll call Rudi's—"

Angie quickly dialed Rudi's Luncheonette. "Rudi, this is Angie Matilla. Jennie's home . . . yes, thank God! She just came in by herself. I don't know how she got past without anybody seeing her." She looked at Jennie. "Jennie, didn't you see anybody looking for you?"

"No. . . ."

"She says no. Not yet. I haven't really had time to ask her anything. No, of course, I was upset. Right now I'm more relieved than anything. I'm just glad to have her back safe and sound. What? Oh . . . thank you, Rudi. That's what I was calling about. Thank you so much. All right. Good-bye."

Angie replaced the receiver and returned to Jennie. "It's O.K. Rudi is sending Chiquitín, the little man that works for him, to find Daddy. If he can't find Daddy, Rudi will call back."

Angie wiped Jennie clean and took her into the kitchen.

"Now . . . you tell me what happened that you are so late. You never disobey us, Jennie. I'm very surprised at you."

"Are you still angry, Mommy?"

"No, I'm not angry anymore. But I want you to tell me where you were and what happened."

"I followed a cat into a building and met Captain Nate . . ." Jennie drank a glass of milk.

"What do you mean, you followed a cat? And who is Captain Nate?"

"He's just a nice old man who lost his union card on account of his being in a politics party like the Democracies and Republicans . . . and had to have an operation—"

"Wait—wait a minute," Angie interrupted. "I don't understand you. Start from the very beginning. Now, when I sent you downstairs to play, what did you do?"

"First . . . I was just bouncing my ball and then I went over to the corner . . . not on the avenue, on the other corner . . ." Jennie lowered her eyes. "I know I'm not supposed to go over that far. . . . "

"Don't worry about that now, just go on and tell me everything."

"Mommy, I saw this really cute kitty and she was crying, because she was hungry . . . and that old orange cat was gonna beat her up . . . so she ran away into a building around the corner, across the street. . . ."

As Jennie spoke, Angie interrupted her, trying to fit in the missing pieces.

"So that's all, and Captain Nate took me back to the corner. And then I came upstairs."

Angie remembered the newspaper article and shuddered. "Jennie, did this old man, Captain Nate, did he do anything to you? Did he touch you anywhere, honey? I have to know. It's all right, you can tell me and I won't be angry."

"No . . . only thing is that he showed me his operation, like I told you. Oh, and he asked me to touch it."

"Touch what?"

"His operation. But I wouldn't, Mommy—it looked awful, ugh . . . like a burn, you know?"

"That's all, Jennie? That's all he asked you to touch?"

"Yes."

"All right, then. But you know you mustn't ever, ever do such a thing again."

"Yes."

The front door opened and Rick walked in. "Angie?" he called out.

"Rick—we're in here! Jennie's home, Rick, and everything's all right; she's safe."

Lali

The alarm clock rang. Lali opened her eyes, stretched out her arm, and pushed in the small knob that shut off the noise. She lay back staring at the ceiling. Off in a corner the paint was peeling and a large crack made that section buckle. Every day she cleaned the small chips of paint that fell on the dresser top and floor. She looked over at Rudi's side of the bed. He was gone. Each morning he awoke at five thirty and, except for Sunday, reset the alarm at seven thirty for Lali. On Sunday the store was closed, but Rudi got up at five-thirty anyway; he had been doing this for sixteen years. Since he always awoke be-

fore the alarm went off, Lali wondered why he bothered
to set the clock, and had asked him about it.

"It's for that one time I might oversleep. Then what
happens to the business and my customers, eh? All waiting for breakfast and no Rudi. No, I don't take chances."

Rudi was down in the luncheonette by six every morning, starting preparations for breakfast and waiting for
the food deliveries. His customers would begin to come
in after seven.

Lali pulled the covers tightly around her neck and
shoulders. The old radiators hissed and clanked, sending
out vaporous heat. In spite of all the noise and steam, the
room remained cold. The heat seemed to escape right
through the walls of the tenement, disappearing into the
street, leaving behind cold moisture which framed the
window panes with a smoky hue and formed sweat drops
on the walls.

Now that it was almost winter again, it was getting
more difficult for Lali to get out of bed in the morning.
At home it was always so easy; with the sound of the
first rooster crowing, she would open her eyes and start
the day.

Lali sighed and closed her eyes; then half opening
them, she squinted. There it was . . . coming into focus.
She saw the morning mist settling like puffs of smoke
scattered over the range of mountains that surrounded the
entire countryside. Sharp mountainous peaks and curves
covered with many shades of green foliage that changed
constantly from light to dark, intense or soft tones, de-

pending on the time of day and the direction of the rays
of the brilliant tropical sun. Ah, the path, she smiled,
following the road that led to her village. Lali inhaled
the sweet and spicy fragrance of the flower gardens that
sprinkled the countryside in abundance. In her mountain
village, as well as in every mountain village on the island
of Puerto Rico, country folk prided themselves on their
flower gardens, which surrounded even the most modest
and humble homes. Oh, Papi's flower garden! There
were bright yellows, scarlet and crimson hues, brilliant
blues, wild purples; every color imaginable flourished on
the plants and shrubbery that blossomed in her father's
flower garden. Lali enjoyed the soft, cool, gentle morning
breeze as she stood by the road and dug her bare feet into
the dark moist earth.

"Lali! Lali, nena, come here! What are you dreaming
about? Always dreaming when there's work to be done.
Papi wants to plant a row of four mango trees over by
the chicken coop. Caramba! We have to prepare the
earth . . ."

Her mother was always calling her, interrupting her
dreams. Her private dreams. She used to wonder what was
going on beyond the mountains, in other places far from
her village. What were people like out there?

Outside in the street, Lali heard the trucks changing
gears; buses and cars honked their horns. Lali opened
her eyes and shivered, feeling a lump in her throat. She
felt the tears coming to her eyes. I'm not gonna cry; it
just makes me tired. Besides, she would be going home

soon. In February, Rudi would close the luncheonette for two weeks. He had promised Lali that for their second wedding anniversary they would vacation in Puerto Rico and she could spend time with her family.

"This is the middle of November . . ." Lali whispered, "so, then December, January, and February! Thank God." She made the sign of the cross. Feeling better, she climbed out of bed, grabbed her bathrobe, and got ready to go to work.

Lali put on her uniform, brushed her hair, tied it back, and applied some lipstick. Quickly she reached in the dresser drawer and took out a pair of slacks and a blouse, slipping them on a plastic hanger. It was Thursday, and she had night school this evening. It saved time if she changed downstairs in the back room before going to class; and Rudi would have less to complain about. She locked the front door and realized she had forgotten her books. Going back into the apartment, Lali remembered she had been so excited about her trip home that she had not completed tonight's assignment. This had never happened before. School and homework were the two things she looked forward to. Well, it doesn't matter, Lali shrugged; Chiquitín will help me finish my homework.

After a lifetime of separation from his mother and family, Chiquitín had been reunited with them over a year ago. That had been the happiest day of his life. He was introduced to his half-sister and half-brothers, stepfather, niece, nephew, and brother-in-law. It took some time for his family to get over the embarrassment of his dwarfishness. Chiquitín was used to people reacting in this way, and set out to prove he would be no burden. Once it was obvious that he would give more than he took, they accepted him completely. Immediately, he had been drawn to Lali, first by her sadness and then by her sense of helplessness.

They were both starting second year English together. Lali was fluent and when she spoke, she no longer planned her sentences ahead of time, or worried about her accent.

Lali walked into the luncheonette, and as usual Rudi had set out her breakfast on the counter. No matter how busy it was, Rudi insisted she have her breakfast undisturbed.

"What happened, Lali? You're fifteen minutes late."

"I'm sorry. I'll hurry up—"

"No," Rudi interrupted, "take your time. I was only worried that something happened . . . take your time. You feeling tired?"

"No." Lali turned away from Rudi and sat down to eat.

She finished breakfast and began the day's work. Lali worked at the grill during the early morning and late evening rush. The rest of the time she cooked the standard meals listed on the menu and the blue plate special of the day.

Rudi had taught her how to cook quite a number of dishes, and how to prepare food for the restaurant business. Lali knew that his first wife had also done most of the cooking. Rudi had told her that they had both worked and saved their money until they were able to buy the luncheonette sixteen years ago. She had seen his first wife's picture in an old photograph album Rudi stored away in a suitcase. Lali had been surprised to see Rudi as a young man, with a full head of dark hair, lean and muscular in an army uniform. He stood with his arm around a young woman who smiled happily. A large orchid corsage was pinned on her brightly flowered print dress. On the back of the photo someone had written, *Carmin and Rudi Padillo on their wedding day—April 19, 1946, Brooklyn, N.Y.* That was the year she had been born; her birthday was a month later, May 3, 1946. Carmin Padillo had died of diabetes and heart complications five years ago. Three years after his first wife's death, Rudi went to Puerto Rico and brought back his second wife, Lali, a twenty-two-year-old bride.

Lali had suffered from shyness all her life, and even as an adult could not overcome the feeling that she must somehow stay out of other people's way. Except for a few trips to San Juan, the capital, she spent most of her life in the village where she was born. One younger brother was still home. All her other brothers and sisters were married. Most lived close to her parents and all of them were in Puerto Rico. Lali had graduated from first year high school and then worked at home helping her mother and father with their small farm and the younger children. Later she worked part-time, helping in the kitchen and waiting on tables in a small tourist road café near the state park a few miles from her home.

Rudi and his first wife had never had children. All his close relatives lived in Puerto Rico. Upon arriving in New York, Lali found herself in a strange environment without anyone to talk to except Rudi. Lali was unable to understand or speak the language she heard. Although they had taught English in the schools back home, it was almost impossible for her to understand what people said. They spoke so rapidly that she could barely make out a word now and then. She had begun her life in this new land in February; the weather was cold and bitter. Lali had never experienced such cold temperatures. Even the snow was a disappointment to her. In books and in the movies she remembered how beautiful everything looked: white, sparkling, and shiny. All her life she had wanted to see and touch snow, but as soon as the snow fell, traffic and pollution turned it to a brown and murky slush.

After almost two years of living and working together, the marriage still proved to be a strain on both Lali and Rudi. Although kind, Rudi was not an affectionate man by nature. He was hard-working and practical, unable to see beyond someone's most obvious need. He had been nervous with his young wife and responded to her shyness with confusion. As a result he developed a taciturn manner with Lali, causing her to withdraw even further into herself. He hoped that a trip back home to Puerto Rico might help lessen the tension between them.

Customers and people in the neighborhood had often kidded Rudi about overworking Lali. At first he had ignored them, but after a while, he wondered if that might not be the cause of the problem between them. When Old Mary's son had come looking for work, Rudi had given him a part-time job helping out during the evenings.

"Mira, Lali, I'm getting extra help. . . . This way, you can take it a little easy now and then, eh?"

Lali had responded indifferently. The harder and longer she worked, the less homesick she felt. There was less time to think; the days were easier to live through and, at night, she was too tired to care.

But Chiquitín made a difference in Lali's life. He was interested in her and showed concern. Slowly she began to talk to Chiquitín, opening up about her loneliness.

"My parents didn't force me to marry him. It was all my idea. I was the one that said yes, even though Rudi was a lot older than me. In fact, he's a year younger than Papi. That's why they told me to think it over. But somehow, he was different, not like the boys I was used to dating. You know, to me he looked like he knew more about the world and all. And then, too, many people back home tell you how wonderful life is here. There's television and the movies; they give another impression. Anyway, I never been glamorous or anything like that, and when Rudi proposed, I couldn't believe it. I saw a chance to get away—to see what was going on in other places, to live in New York, another kind of life. It just seemed exciting to me. Now, Chiquitín, I have no life, except work and more work and church on Sunday, and nobody to talk to. I miss everybody. You know, I can't talk to people too easy. With you it's different because we are both from the countryside, I guess. But I don't understand what's going on around me."

"Come on, Lali, enroll in school with me," Chiquitín had said. "It's wonderful, you can learn the language and you won't feel like that, so left out . . ."

"But I was never a good student," she had protested.

"No matter. I'm not so good myself," he had insisted, "but I'll help you. Together we'll learn. What do you say? You are not doing nothing else. Why not try, eh?"

After she enrolled in school, there were days and sometimes even weeks when she did not feel depressed. It was only recently, now that the holidays were near, that Lali felt homesick again.

This evening she finished her tasks, working extra hard so that she could leave everything ready for the evening's rush of customers. Lali waited for Chiquitín to come in so that they could leave for class together.

Promptly at six thirty, Chiquitín walked in.

"I'm ready; just let me get my books," Lali called out to him.

"Lali, wait . . . " Chiquitín walked over to her. "I can't make it to class tonight."

"What? Why?"

"My brother Federico is coming home. My mother got a phone call this afternoon and we have to pick him up at the airport. He's coming in from California for the holidays."

"Oh, I didn't know."

"Nobody knew; it was a surprise. You heard me talk

about him, right? I mean, I never met him, but Mami talks a lot about him."

"When is he getting here?"

"At eight thirty this evening. I gotta go right away. Ramón is waiting for me."

"O.K."

"You can manage all right without me, can't you, Lali?"

"Sure. You know, this is the first time you missed class. But, please, Chiquitín, go on; don't worry. I'll give you the homework assignment when I see you tomorrow." Lali smiled at him. "Go on, have a good time."

"Let me tell Rudi I can't be in tonight . . . " Chiquitín went over to Rudi and explained.

"It's O.K., Chiquitín, go on, meet your brother. I'll get Raquel Martínez if it gets too busy, but I don't think so; it's been a little slow this week anyway. Go on, and say hello to your brother from us."

Quickly Chiquitín left.

"Lali, can you get to school all right by yourself?" Rudi approached her. "It's all right?"

"Of course it's all right. I know the way." Lali got her books.

"Imagine, he never saw his own brother. Ave María, but then, he never met his own mother until a year ago." Rudi shook his head.

"He couldn't help that. He was an infant when she left him in Puerto Rico."

"Nobody is saying it's his fault; I just mean it's a funny

thing, two brothers, grown men, and they don't even know each other, that's all."

"Well"—Lali put on her coat—"they'll know each other soon. His brother is getting here in a couple of hours."

"I wonder if they gonna look alike, eh?" He smiled at her.

Lali glared angrily at Rudi, then lowered her eyes and shrugged. "I don't know." She disliked jokes or innuendos about Chiquitín's dwarfishness.

"Wait a minute. I don't mean alike about his size or nothing. I mean his face . . . if they look alike! You know, brothers and all?"

"I gotta go."

"I can't talk to her . . . " Rudi mumbled after she had left. "Nothing I say is right."

Customers walked in.

"Hey, Rudi, what's good to eat tonight?" a man called out.

"What do you mean, what's good? Everything is good . . . here in Rudi's, everything's the best!"

"Ta . . . ta . . . takata . . . sabes que te quiero . . . mi corazón!" Federico finished the last line of the bolero. He sang as he worked, setting up what was needed for counter service. Turning he looked at Lali, who had been staring at him. He winked, and twirling a dry dishcloth, snapped it playfully at her. "Got you!"

"Federico!" Lali screamed and laughed as she ducked. "Stop being so silly. Honestly, you are worse than a baby!"

"Your baby, Mami?" he smiled.

Lali blushed and turned away. Federico walked up to her and placed his hands on the nape of her neck, gently massaging it. Lali closed her eyes and leaned against him for a moment, then quickly drew back.

"We better stop; somebody might come in, or see us."

It was still early and quiet in the luncheonette. No one was about.

"Nobody is coming in right now; relax. Besides, we ain't doing nothing outrageous, just being friendly."

"Federico!" Lali shook her head, and playfully poked him. "He's coming down today, you know," she spoke in a serious tone, "at around three this afternoon. He's staying for a little while. He can manage with the cane a lot better and he walks on the heel of his cast. Yesterday he practiced going down the steps and today's he gonna make it down here."

"It'll still be a while before he can take over again . . . "

"I know, but what will we do when he comes back, Federico?"

"Don't worry about that now, will you, baby? One step at a time. Right now things are fine, O.K.? Let's not go spoiling it."

Lali nodded and went into the back to begin preparation of the day's cooked meals.

It had been two weeks since the accident.

"What miserable luck, eh?" Rudi had shouted. "Done in by that old bastard of a cat! I said I would kill him if I caught him near the garbage cans again, and damn, if he didn't get me first! ¡Hijo de puta! Tsk." Rudi had gone out late one evening to chase the old orange alley cat away from the garbage. He ran after it with an empty beer bottle and slipped on some rotten fruit that had been thrown in the gutter. Rudi had been able to get up and limp back to the store, but the pain in his right leg made it impossible for him to stand.

The doctor had put a cast on his broken leg and told him that he would have to stay home, immobile, for at least two weeks. When Rudi had protested, the doctor insisted.

"You have no choice. You're not a youngster. With a man your age, things take longer to heal. Mr. Padillo, you are fifty-five, not twenty-five anymore. Patience, that's what will help you get better. In fact, it's the only thing we older folks should learn to be best at, being patient."

Rudi had been furious. "I'm gonna get my thirty-eight and when I see that cat, I'll shoot that son of a bitch . . . lo juro! I swear on my mother's grave!"

He kept a thirty-eight caliber pistol in the luncheonette. He had not been robbed for over a year, but he was not taking chances.

Rudi often said, "You can't leave it to luck, not in this city, you can't," as he polished and cleaned his gun, keeping it handy. "Just in case" was his philosophy.

"What am I gonna do about my business?" he had said to Lali. "You can't run it yourself, all alone. Dios mío, if I shut down now for two weeks, that's our vacation and trip to Puerto Rico."

When Chiquitín had suggested his brother Federico as an alternative to shutting down the luncheonette, Lali had jumped at the idea.

"Rudi, please let's try. I want this trip back home more than anything, please." She never asked for very much, and although Rudi was reluctant at the idea of someone else running his business, he agreed. Secretly he hoped Lali would see this as an act of caring on his part, and that it would bring her closer to him.

"How much experience does he have?" Chiquitín told him that Federico had worked in the restaurant business for many years. "Wait a minute, I thought you said he was a singer and songwriter and all that! How come now he's a counter man?"

"He is a singer and a songwriter, but he can't always make a living at that. So he supports himself by working in the restaurant business. Honest, Rudi," Chiquitín had persisted, "he's got lots of experience. We been talking about it. He's worked in Los Angeles, Vegas, Denver, Chicago, Miami, all over. He's out of work now, so I know he'll be glad to do it."

"O.K. then, I give it a try. But only for a few days, and then we decide more."

That was how it all had started. Federico knew the restaurant business well. The customers were satisfied and Rudi had no complaints.

This morning, as she worked in back, Lali looked at Federico through the open serving counter. She loved his straight tall form and the way his dark hair fell gently over his wide forehead. He moved quickly and gracefully. She felt herself tremble. She wanted to be near him all the time, every minute if possible. Lali recalled that when she first met him she had been struck by his facial resemblance to Chiquitín. Federico was dark and Chiquitín was so blond and fair; yet, they had the same smile and many similar mannerisms. Even their tone of voice was similar.

Lali had volunteered to get up at five thirty from the beginning, so that she could teach Federico where things were and he could learn the routine of the luncheonette quickly. She still got up at five thirty, but it was so that she could spend more time with Federico.

It had not taken very long for Lali and Federico to become lovers. Her attraction to him had become stronger and stronger, and on the third day, when he approached her, Lali was very ready. She accepted his affection with a desperation and fierceness that had unnerved Federico. But her naive responses to his lovemaking made him a very gentle lover and protective toward her.

"Lali," he had whispered, "you are like a virgin . . . you don't know nothing."

"I know I love you Federico. I love you more than anything in this whole world. Teach me, I'll do whatever you say."

By the end of the first week, Chiquitín suspected their relationship. That feeling of closeness and trust that had seemed a natural part of his relationship with Lali disappeared. Chiquitín watched Lali carefully, catching the way she blushed when she was near Federico as well as the nuances in the smiles and glances she directed his way. She avoided Chiquitín's eyes and responded either abruptly or vaguely to his questions and attempts at conversation, treating him as an intruder. She told Chiquitín that she would not be able to continue in night school with him.

"I can't go until Rudi comes back. I have to stay and help Federico."

"It's O.K. Don't worry. I'll take down the assignments for you. And I'll help you with them, so that you don't fall behind in class."

"No, never mind, Chiquitín. Right now I'm too busy to worry about that. Besides, I might not go back to class at all . . . I'm not sure."

Chiquitín was used to confiding and sharing his dreams with Lali. Often they would reminisce about Puerto Rico, expressing how much they both missed their beloved island.

"Ave María . . . do you know that now it's the best season for quenepas in Puerto Rico? Chiquitín, can you taste them? What I would give for just one taste of that delicious pungent fruit, picked right off a branch. Madre!"

"You know, Lali, maybe I can go back someday. Start a small business myself. I don't think I want my mother to die here. She feels as I do, and says she wants to go back home."

When Lali took Federico as her lover, she shattered a part of Chiquitín's world.

Federico Cortez was the apple of Old Mary's eye, her favorite son.

"That one, he's too damned handsome for his own good! Women will be the death of him. I've told him, mi hijito, listen, you got women too much on the brain. But he don't listen. I say, stay home, settle down, raise a family like your sister Chela. He only wants to write songs and sing, Ave María. Well, but he's got talent—no luck, but good looks and talent. Pobre, what can one expect, eh? Women run after him. Really, that's his problem. Also, he don't wanna be serious. Listen, I'm lucky if I see my son Federico once every five years, and I never know where he is. One day he's gonna come home and find Old Mary dead and buried! I talk to him plenty, but it don't do no good."

Everybody liked Federico; he was open, warm, generous, and easy to be with. His passion was for singing the songs he wrote.

"The breaks have been against me all along, man. I get my songs to be played here and there, you know, when I get me a gig. The band will play them, with my own arrangements and all, but I can't get published. You know how hard it is for Latin music to get published anyway, right? So dig, I write the songs in Spanish and in English, still . . . zero! No way they gonna let me in the door. Wait, let me sing this new ballad for you. Just a couple of lines, listen . . . "

Federico was always willing to sing a few bars, showing off the lyrics and tune of the new song he had just written.

"Man, bro . . . " He had confided to Chiquitín, "I'm already thirty-two, thirty-two! I don't know how long I'm gonna go on, you know? A man gets tired of running and sleeping here and there; no roots of his own. But somehow I keep on. You know what keeps me going? Writing songs! I swear that's my life . . . my life, man. When I'm up there singing what I wrote, that music is playing, and people are listening to me—that's living! That's when I come to life. That's what it's all about, dig?"

When Chiquitín first decided to speak to Federico about Lali, his devotion to his mother and family made him feel unsure and uneasy. Federico was his brother, and after all, the favorite son. Besides, he told himself, what's it to me what they do. It's no business of mine. But that look of adoration for Federico in Old Mary's eyes was also there when he looked at Lali; and he began to dislike his brother, resenting his ease and self-assurance.

"Smug bastard," he had half-whispered as he watched Federico looking at Lali.

Chiquitín had learned early that because he was physically different from the average person, life for him would have limits. From the simple tasks of buying clothing that fit, traveling on public transportation, reaching for objects on high counters, being able to speak face to face with people without being ignored, to the more serious problems of getting a job, commanding respect as an adult, and speaking another language, life for Chiquitín was a series of obstacles to be overcome. But he had managed, and managed well, he thought, until Lali. Now he realized he was deeply in love with her and this thought angered and confused him. Lali had never shown that she was interested in him except as a friend. And he had always approached her with the respect due a married woman. As Federico's lover, Lali was different and he knew he was losing her. He's not in love with Lali . . . he's only using her, Chiquitín thought. He felt a rage against Federico. He planned to speak to him, have it out with Federico. One night after work, Chiquitín had spoken to his brother.

"Take care . . . Federico, Lali is not one of your quick one-night stands. She's not like that! I know her. She's a very serious person. I don't know what you're after or what you want, but—"

"What are you talking about?" Federico interrupted, protesting. "You are jumping to some heavy conclusions. Hey, man, remember me? Your brother, who don't get serious with nobody. I got me my career . . . and I don't get involved with nothing I can't handle."

"Federico, I'm older than you and I know. I know what I'm saying to you. I see. I'm not blind to what's going on. Now, don't bullshit me."

The two men stared at each other in silence for a moment.

"O.K." Federico nodded, lit a cigarette and exhaled, looking at Chiquitín. "So what? We ain't harming nobody . . . all right? What you worried about? Her old man is a dud; he's old enough to be her grandfather. He fires blanks, O.K.? What should she do? Be a nun? Come on!"

Chiquitín lowered his eyes, unable to speak.

"Hey, mira, Chiquitín, man, you got a case on her, right? If that's so, why didn't you tell me. You're a sneaky little mother, coño! Pero, why didn't you let me know? I could've stayed cool, you know, keep off the merchandise!"

"No." Chiquitín looked up at his brother. "She's not my . . . my lover, it's nothing to do with me. It's that she's my friend. I don't want her hurt, that's all!"

"You got no problems then, right? We're just having fun. I swear to you, that's all! She knows it and I know it."

"She's married, you know, and her husband is your employer, Federico. He's doing you a favor, remember that. And he's also a nice guy."

"I know . . . and I just told you, Rudi ain't doing nothing for her. O.K., so he's doing me a favor and I'm doing him a favor!" Federico snickered and waited for Chiquitín to respond. "Come on, man, he don't know what's happening. He's only worried about his business, and I'm taking care of that too! I'm taking care of all his business, right?" Federico looked at his brother good-humoredly.

"To you it's all a joke, right?" Chiquitín shook his head.

"Come on, will you . . . Rudi don't know what's happening. So what's the harm? You know something, Chiquitín? You too moral. I seen that when I met you, and you worry too much. All this business about married women and all. She's got needs and I got needs, that's all." Federico shrugged, "That's it!"

"How do you feel about her . . . Lali?"

"Look, she's nice. She's really a good person. You know? I like her a lot. Lali is doing her thing and I'm doing mine. Now, why do you have to make a big deal out of all this?" Federico sighed. "All right?"

"Promise me one thing, O.K.?" Chiquitín spoke very slowly and deliberately, looking at Federico. "I'm asking this as your brother. Don't mess her up. She's not used to . . . what's going on, eh? Don't mess her up! This is what I ask from you. I want you to promise this to me, as my brother."

"I promise. Hey! Is that all? Man, I promise. Look, I'm cool . . . she's cool, O.K.? Brother, you ain't got nothing to worry about, te lo juro. I swear." Federico lifted his right hand.

"I wanna believe you, Federico."

"Hey? Would I lie to you? After I said I promised?" Federico extended his right hand, holding out an open palm. "Give me five on that and we'll seal the promise."

"O.K." Chiquitín slapped the open palm. In spite of his doubts, he found himself smiling and listening to his brother.

"This one's a beauty. Mira, I'm gonna sing just a couple of lines. This new song is—it's tremendous, baby! Tremendo . . . listen to this . . . "

By the end of the third week Rudi managed, with the aid of a cane and by taking a step at a time very slowly, to climb down the flight of stairs by himself. He spent several hours a day in the luncheonette, making sure his customers were satisfied.

At first he noticed that Lali had a healthy glow about her, was even-tempered and friendlier than usual. But as the week went by, she became more and more irritable and hardly spoke to Rudi at all. When he announced that his cast was coming off a week earlier than expected, and that he would be spending more time in the luncheonette, Lali could barely keep from crying.

Rudi decided that it was Lali's homesickness and her desire to visit Puerto Rico that caused her behavior. That evening he mentioned it to Federico and Chiquitín.

"It's only because she misses her family so much. She's anxious about the trip we gonna take back to Puerto Rico. She can't wait."

"Sure! You're right!" Federico agreed. "Women can be moody like that and about no big thing at all, believe me. You'll see, she'll get over it once she gets home."

"Well, I'm glad you're taking her home, Rudi." Chiquitín looked at Federico, who avoided his eyes. "It will be good for Lali. Listen, we better get you upstairs, it's time to go."

Every evening Chiquitín helped Rudi up the flight of stairs and into his apartment. As they walked up, Rudi spoke to Chiquitín.

"You probably miss Puerto Rico, too, eh?"

"All my family's here, so I don't miss it in the way Lali does. Pero . . . yes, I miss Puerto Rico very much in other ways. You know, the climate and the country-side, especially where I spent most of my life. You know the town of Aibonito, yes? Well, then you know how beautiful it is in that section of the island. And I miss the language, the people—yes, in many ways I miss my country."

"Well," Rudi said, stopping every once in a while to catch his breath, "I can't say I miss Puerto Rico. You see, I been here since I got my discharge in 1946 from the army. I married my first wife here. I love Nueva York . . . it's my home. I go to Puerto Rico, and I can't take the slow pace there no more. Nuyorquino . . . that's me now. Even though Puerto Rico has changed since when I was young, what with all them hotels and tourism and everything. Still, here is where my life and my business is, and my people. Yes, this Nueva York is my home. But I know for Lali it's not the same, for her it's difficult." Rudi stopped speaking, shook his head and then looked at Chiquitín, speaking in a low voice. "I don't mind tell-ing you in confidence . . . nothing I do pleases that woman. I don't know if marrying such a young girl was a right thing to do. Oh, there are things I can't complain about. Like she works hard . . . you know how hard-working she is. In that way I've got myself a gem of a woman but . . ." Rudi sighed. "It's not right between us. I know she don't think so, but I . . . I love Lali, you know? When I first seen her I knew there was something

146

about her I liked. She seemed so anxious to get away from where she was, like some sort of caged bird . . . and she was so young and innocent, very timid in a way. Although, now that I know her I know she's strong willed. I mean, she appears timid, but she's got a mind of her own, all right. Anyway, I was attracted to her, maybe it's because me and my first wife never had kids of our own. Sometimes I feel more like her father than her husband. I don't know, sometimes, Chiquitín . . . I don't know what to do to please her."

"Rudi, you're taking her home, eh? That will make things better, you'll see."

"That's right! But now with this damned accident, it's only made matters worse. Of course, thank God you recommended your brother. Federico has been a good help. Listen, I appreciate it. I'm not an ungrateful person. I mean, to get somebody like him on short notice and all. And now we can take our trip to Puerto Rico! That Federico, he's O.K. in my book."

"Soon you will be taking over again anyway, Rudi, and remember, Federico will be on his way. He's not serious about settling down or nothing. He likes to move, what with his career and all . . ."

"Sure, he didn't ask me to stay on or nothing, so I guess he'll be leaving. I mean, I ain't got full-time work for him. Even now, my giving him a full salary is hard. I have to take a loss, but it's been worth it!"

That night after they closed the store and Chiquitín left, Lali spoke to Federico.

"Federico, I can't stand him, I can't. Don't you see?"

"Take it easy on him, Lali; Rudi ain't done nothing."

"He's here every day! That's what he's done, and he's coming back soon! Can't you see? He won't need you anymore, then what? He'll be back. Federico . . ." Lali began to cry. "Tell me what to do."

"Come on now, baby." Federico embraced Lali, holding her still for a moment. "Calm down."

"How can I calm down? He's coming back to spoil everything!"

"Lali, sooner or later you knew he was coming back, right? So now it's happened."

"What do you mean, it's happened? It's happened! What about us?"

"We'll go right on seeing each other. Don't worry, baby."

"How?" Lali pushed him away. "How? I work from morning to night . . . six days a week in this stinking place. I'm never out of his sight—how? And where will you be? Will you go away? Federico . . ."

"We'll manage something, Mami. Don't worry."

"Federico . . ." Lali looked at him, swallowed, and tried not to cry. "Take me with you. Take me wherever you go. Please . . . oh, please!"

"Hey,"—Federico turned away—"you know I can't do that."

"Please, oh, please, don't leave me here with him, please . . ." Lali paused. Federico had his back to her and she waited for a response. He didn't answer. "I'll work, I won't be no burden or no trouble to you. I promise, I'll do whatever you say . . . anything you ask." Lali drew a breath and screamed, *"Pleeease!"* She wrapped her arms around Federico, holding him as tightly as she could, pressing her head against his back. "Don't you see? If you didn't come along, I wouldn't know what it's like to . . . to love somebody like I love you. Now . . . now I can't stand him no more. I hate him! I'll work and you can stay home and write your songs. You'll see. This way you won't have to work, and you can devote your whole time to songwriting. Please . . . answer me . . . Federico. I'm begging you, querido, mi alma, my soul —don't leave me." Lali began to whimper.

"Oh, man, Lali." Federico released himself from Lali's grip and turned to face her. You know I never promised to take you with me, or nothing, right? We never even discussed any of that. Now you're taking advantage of me, you know that! You ain't playing fair."

"Federico . . ." Lali sobbed quietly. "Federico, what do I have to do? Tell me what I have to do, and I'll do it. Just let me be with you. You even said you were tired of running around with no place to call home. I can give you that home, work for you, take care of you."

"I said all that before I spent three weeks in this place working like a mule. I always say that, but I don't mean it. I'll never give up my life singing and writing songs. And there's something else you should know, I ain't giving up my freedom, baby—no way!"

"You don't have to. You can do what you want, honest! Look, Federico, I got money, yes! I got some money saved, and I can get more—money to help you get started. You always say, if you had money, you would publish your own songs. Maybe you can do it."

"How much money you got?"

"Five hundred dollars of my own. It's yours, all yours."

"Five hundred dollars ain't nothing, anyway; it don't—"

"I can get more, much more."

"Where?"

"Rudi and I have money in a joint bank account. I can get it out."

"How much?"

"Five thousand dollars. And, we can take at least a week's receipts with us. Now that he's got the cast, I take the money to the bank. I just won't make the deposits. I'll hold the money. It's my money, too; I've earned it. That's a good start, eh? And my five hundred, too."

"I don't know." Federico looked at Lali, hesitating. "I'm not sure about this, you know?"

"I'm sure. I'm sure enough for the both of us. Honest, de veras—we can do it. It will be so easy."

"When?"

"Soon. We have to do it very soon, before he gets that cast off his leg. With the cast on a leg, how far can he go, eh?"

"I don't know, baby, it's very risky, you know? I mean, he's a shrewd old dude. He might make a lotta trouble for us."

"How? If we're gone, how? We can buy a car. We got enough money. You said you needed a car. And then we can get away, out of the state. You know, all the places you told me about . . . we can go there. He won't know where we are. Then you can get your songs published."

"Let me think this through first."

"Federico, there's nothing to think about. Let's just do it. All we have to—"

"Lali!" he interrupted. "You don't know anything about life out there. You don't know what you'd be getting into, O.K.? It's rough out there, and life with me ain't gonna be no picnic. Besides, I don't like to be tied down."

"But . . . life without you is not possible for me no longer, can't you see that, Federico? Federico, I'll follow you, I will. You can't leave me here—you can't!" She clung to him.

"All right, we'll do it, but I don't promise you nothing."

"Oh, Federico, you won't be sorry. I promise you with all my heart. I'll make you happy!"

"Shh . . . sh . . . it's O.K., be cool. Now, we have to plan this out just right . . ."

The day they planned to leave was the Friday of the fourth week after the accident. All week Lali had pretended to go to the bank to deposit the receipts of the previous day. This morning she did go to the bank, not to make a deposit, but to withdraw five thousand dollars from the joint bank account and five hundred dollars from her personal savings. She put two thousand dollars in a separate envelope, just as Federico had instructed her. Lali gave the envelope to Federico, and that afternoon he made an excuse, leaving for two hours. He said he had to see an agent about a singing job for the holidays at a small club. Actually, he had gone to buy a car so that they could leave that night.

Lali had already packed a few things in a small suitcase and hidden it in back of the store. She was nervous that day, almost giddy. For the first time since her decision to leave Rudi, she thought about her family and the trip she wouldn't be taking back home. She was ashamed to think of what her parents would say. They would understand if they knew Federico; he was all that mattered.

Lali looked around at the luncheonette, wondering where she would be tomorrow or the next day, or the next? Away from here . . . away from him, she thought. A familiar feeling came over her and she remembered how she had once dreamed of another life before she had left her home; Lali shuddered. Nevermind, this is different, I'm going with the man I love. She shook off the sense of apprehension.

When Federico returned, Rudi asked him how it went.

"Fabuloso . . . man, I got me a fine gig for after I finish here. In a small club way out on Long Island. No big deal, but what the hell, they'll play my songs, and that's what it's all about."

Lali watched him as he spoke and smiled. He was so

convincing she almost believed him. She had told him
once that he was a great actor.

"You ought to get a prize. I don't know how you can
stay so cool around Rudi. Doesn't it bother you?" Federico had laughed, and responded, "What you don't
know, don't hurt! Right?"

That evening, more than ever, Lali avoided Chiquitín's
eyes. She wanted to tell him she was leaving, realizing
that she would miss him very much. After all, Chiquitín
was her only real friend. And when she had asked
Federico, he had warned her not to say a word.

"You crazy . . . outta your mind? Baby, it could mean
our lives. That old man of yours got a thirty-eight. Now
I know that sucker will use it if he gets any info on us,
dig? So cool, Lali, we gotta stay real cool and tight. This
is between you and me, nobody else! No Chiquitín, you
hear?"

Somehow, it didn't seem right to leave and not say a
word to her friend. I'll write to him in time, and let him
know where we are. He'll come to visit us; after all,
they're brothers. Chiquitín will be part of our family
and welcomed in our home. I'll make it up to him. She
sighed, feeling better.

Chiquitín helped Rudi upstairs, and when he returned
to the luncheonette, Lali and Federico were busy tending
to the night customers. Everything seemed normal.

After Chiquitín left, they closed the store. Lali went
into the back, returning with the rest of the money.

"Federico, here it is. What kind of car did you get?"

"Oh, a sixty-nine Mustang, in great condition—bright red, real nice."

"Here," she handed him the money.

"Listen, baby, you keep that safe in your handbag. Now, here's what I want you to do. I'm gonna get the car and drive it closer, not too close, but close enough so we can split fast, O.K.?"

"All right . . ."

"You wait here for me. I'll be back within the hour."

"Why so long?"

"I gotta go get the car checked, fill it with gas, and get ready to split. Hey! Things gotta be done right!"

"O.K., don't be cross with me, please. I love you so much, I don't wanna be separated from you no more. I'm so happy!"

"Sure, O.K. But, I gotta leave now, so remember, I'll be back in an hour. Lock up after me."

"Federico, I love you." Lali smiled.

"Yeah, me too. Let me get going."

Because she had nothing else to do, Lali continued to work, cleaning and setting up things for the following day.

From time to time she checked the clock, and an hour later when there was a knock at the door, Lali was startled. Federico used his key, he wouldn't knock. She was afraid of burglars, and very cautiously pulled back the shade. She saw Chiquitín. Lali unlocked the door, opening it partially.

"What are you doing here?"

"Lali, I have to talk to you."

"I can't talk to you now, Chiquitín, it's too late at night. Can't it wait till tomorrow?"

"Please, Lali, let me come inside. I have something for you." Chiquitín held up an envelope. "It's from . . . Federico."

"What?" Lali stepped back into the store.

Chiquitín walked in and locked the door. "Here."

Lali opened the envelope and read the enclosed note:

Dear Lali:

I can't do it baby, I just can't. I tried, but I know it won't work. I took the money for the car, but as soon as I get myself straight, I'll send back every penny. You have my word on that. Lali, you will find some-one else. That's the way life goes. You are a fine per-son and a good girl, you deserve better than me.

Yours,
Federico

"This is not true! Where did you get this? Tell me, you made it up, right? Tell me!"

"Federico gave it to me about an hour ago. He told me to wait till now. That's why I came down."

Lali slumped into a booth. She put her arms on the table, and leaning forward, buried her head. After a long moment she sat up and looked at Chiquitín.

"I can't cry, Chiquitín. Maybe it's because I don't be-lieve it. That he's gone."

Chiquitín sat down opposite her. "Lali, you're better off, believe me. He couldn't make you happy. He don't love you. Listen, he's too selfish. If you want to change your life, you can do it, but not like this. It's not right."

"Do you know where Federico went?"

"No."

"If I knew where he went, I would follow him. I would beg him to take me with him. I would do anything for Federico. I don't care." Lali lowered her eyes. "Are you ashamed of me, Chiquitín? That I can be this way?"

"No, of course I'm not. What are you saying?"

"You don't know how it is, Chiquitín. I'm so in love with him that it doesn't even matter if he don't love me back. You don't know what it's like to love someone so much. It hurts to think about him. Just to be near him, to see him, that's all I asked. It wasn't so much . . ." Lali's voice faltered and her eyes filled with tears. She began to cry openly, sobbing. Chiquitín stepped out of the booth and sat beside her. "Oh, Chiquitín, what shall I do? Federico . . . Federico . . . help me."

Slowly he put his arms around her and she leaned against him, crying softly. He stroked her hair.

"Mira, nena, you'll feel better. It will all heal in time. I know how it hurts, too, you know . . . but it just takes a while, you'll see. Lali, honey, calm down. Mami . . . please, love, just relax, that's it, relax . . ."

His voice was soft and it sounded just like Federico's. Lali closed her eyes, embracing Chiquitín. Very gently, he kissed her forehead, her eyes, her cheeks, and then her lips.

"Please," she whispered, "stay with me a while. Don't leave me alone. Please stay . . ."

Quietly Chiquitín put out the lights. When he returned to her, he very slowly and with great tenderness began to caress and make love to Lali.

She responded with gratitude and compassion. In this way, together, they comforted each other.

The
Robbery

PART ONE

Before going down to work that morning, Lali examined
herself carefully in the mirror. For quite some time after
Federico had left, she couldn't bear to look at herself.
He had made her feel beautiful and very special. Lately,
she had begun to feel better about herself, deciding that
she could, after all, live with her plainness. For a moment
she thought of Federico and closed her eyes, realizing she
still felt deeply about him. It was June; six months had
passed since he had left. Not a word had been received;
no one knew of his whereabouts, and she was sure he
would never write to her. Lali shrugged; perhaps it was

just as well, after what happened. Whenever she recalled Rudi's hateful name-calling and threats to send her back home to her family in disgrace, she was overwhelmed with shame.

"Your family should repay me, and give me back the money you stole for that man. They should know who their virgin daughter is. You are worse than a whore! At least they charge . . . but no, you had to give him more than what he expected. What did you plan to do? Clean me out? Steal everything I own and worked for?"

Chiquitín had spoken with Rudi and managed to calm him down. Even Old Mary and Ramón had intervened. They promised Rudi that they would try to get in touch with Federico and as soon as they knew where he was, they would do everything possible to persuade him to return the money.

Rudi finally agreed not to tell Lali's family about Federico or about the money. It took some time, but several weeks later, things were back to normal between Rudi and Lali. They worked hard, worried about the business, and hardly spoke to each other.

And what had happened between her and Chiquitín the night Federico left was never mentioned between them. Chiquitín treated Lali as always, with respect and consideration; and for that she was grateful.

The warm weather outside and the bright sunshine that shone through the bedroom window reminded her once more of Canovanas, the farm in Puerto Rico, and her family. She hoped she could make it up to Rudi somehow, work even harder than she ever had, and earn that trip back home.

Lali glanced at herself in the mirror once more, then finished dressing. Today was Friday and a busy day, especially at night, when customers came in for the blue plate special. She rushed out, afraid of being late.

"Plain grilled . . . B.L.T. without! Fries for one!" Rudi called out the orders to Lali as she worked quickly at the grill. He was so busy serving customers that he did not notice the two teenage boys who had come into the luncheonette and stood nervously by the door. The tall boy had on dark sunglasses and the shorter boy wore a green suede cap with the front brim pulled down almost covering his eyes.

It was near the end of the night rush, and every seat at the counter as well as the three small booths were still occupied.

"There's gonna be a booth empty in a couple of minutes," Chiquitín said to the boys as he cleared dirty dishes, stacking them into the large plastic basin he carried.

"It's O.K., man. We're waiting for the counter," the taller boy answered.

Two booths emptied out, customers paid their checks, and left. The boys stood by silently and waited. Finally three customers left the counter, and the boys sat down.

"O.K., boys," Rudi asked, "what will it be?"

"Gimme a Coke," said the tall boy.

"Gimme the same." The second boy's voice was barely audible.

"You wanna Coke, too, you said?" The boy nodded. "What else you boys want?"

"Nothing." The tall boy looked at his companion, "Carlos, you want something else?" He shook his head. "That's it for us two."

"Large or small?"

"Small, right, Carlos?" His companion nodded.

"Here," Rudi set down two small glasses of Coca-Cola in front of them. "That'll be thirty cents, fifteen apiece."

The tall boy searched in his pockets. "You got change, man?" He turned to his companion.

"Wait a minute, Tommy, I'll see." He dug into his pocket.

"Nevermind now," Rudi said. "Pay on your way out."

Except for the boys, there were only two other customers in the luncheonette now; in a few minutes they left.

Lali, Rudi, and Chiquitín were busy cleaning and putting things away.

"O.K., boys," Rudi said loudly, "we're closing up. Let's go. That's thirty cents for two small Cokes."

"Now!" Tommy yelled. Carlos jumped in front of the door. Tommy held out a hand gun. "O.K., Pops . . . this is a hype! Stickup!" He motioned with his gun. "Step back. . . . Keep your hands up in back of your heads. Up! In back of your heads . . . and nobody's getting hurt."

"What kind of shit you kids trying to pull?" Rudi stepped toward them.

"Cool it, you old motherfucker, or I'll shoot your fucking face in!" Rudi stopped. "Now get back there . . . fast! Fast!" Rudi stepped back with Lali and Chiquitín. "All right, now stay right there in the aisle, between the counter and that last booth. If I see anybody move, I'll shoot! And my partner got you covered . . . so don't get any ideas. Carlos!" Tommy glanced at his companion, "Where the fuck's your piece, man? Get it out, coño!"

Carlos searched in his pockets and pulled out a small hand gun; he held it out nervously. "Now cover these cocksuckers. First one that makes any little bit of a move, we'll blow your brains all over this place! Carlos, you stay by that door . . . don't let nobody in, you hear?" Tommy stepped up to the cash register and opened it. He took out the money, stuffing it into his pockets. Quickly he looked around him, under the counter, on the shelves, and then walked toward the back room. "Just stay cool. . . . Nobody takes a step. Carlos, you watching them?"

"Yeah!"

"Good man!" Tommy hurried into the back kitchen and quickly searched around the shelves and cabinets, pushing over boxes of food and overturning the kitchenware. "Shit, there's nothing in here!" Coming back out, he pointed the gun at Rudi. "O.K., Pops, where's the rest of the money?"

"That's all there is. . . . Take it and get the hell out of here!"

"What you mean that's all there is! Shit! Don't gimme no mierda bullshit, you old fuck! Where's the rest?"

"In the bank where punks like you who don't work can't touch it . . ."

"Hey"—Tommy walked out from behind the counter, moving closer to Rudi—"You old bastard! You want me to put a hole through your face? I know you gotta have more money here."

"Listen," Lali spoke, "he's telling the truth. What you took from the register is all we got. We make bank deposits every day, honest. Listen, don't be doing nothing foolish. . . . You are too young."

"Shut up, miss, O.K.?" Tommy looked at Lali. "I don't wanna be rough with you, so shut up! And you"—he looked at Rudi—"that's all you got? You old shit you, I oughta shoot you . . . you old—"

"Tommy!" Carlos shouted. "Let's get outta here. . . . Let's take what we got and split, man! Before somebody comes in, let's split!"

"Shut up, don't be no faggot with me, punk! We'll leave when I'm ready, O.K.? Now, you two empty out your pockets, right now . . . and put everything here, right on the counter. And take off your watches. You too, shorty . . . I'm talking to you. And take off your ring, Pops. You too, miss, take off your rings, watches, that chain you got on your neck . . . go on! Hurry up or I'll pull it off you." They all did as they were told. Rudi had trouble removing his wedding ring. "Miss, you got a pocketbook, right? Get it, quick . . . and don't do nothing funny or I'll shoot a hole in your old man's gut. Go on!" Lali ran in the back, returning with her handbag. "O.K., miss, just empty it all out, right there on the counter; that's right." Rudi was still struggling to get his wedding ring off. "Get that fucking ring off, will you? Or I'll shoot it off!"

"Just a minute, it's hard to take off. It ain't worth so much anyway. . . . There, there . . ." He stuck his finger in his mouth, moistening the ring until he slipped it off. "There it is!" He threw it on the counter.

Carefully Tommy removed the money from all three wallets while keeping an eye on them. Then he put the money and jewelry in his pockets.

"How old are you, son?" Rudi asked.

"Don't son me. I ain't your son . . . and I'm old enough to shoot your ass off! Lie down on the fucking floor, all of you . . . right here, that's right, lie down. Hurry . . . coño!"

"You ain't getting away with this, you know that? They'll catch you and put you in jail!"

"Good; I like jail, I love it there! I'll get rehabilitated and come out even better, right? Fuck you, mister, and lie down, face down, all three of you, face down. Hands behinds your heads."

They all lay face down between the counter and the booths, with their hands behind their heads, taking up all the floor space.

"Vámonos, man, let's get out of this joint!" Carlos pleaded. "Please, man . . ."

"O.K., we're leaving now, and you people better wait a few minutes." Tommy waved his gun at them. "I didn't get shit here tonight . . . and I'm warning you, the first one comes after us, I'll blow his motherfucking ass sky-high, so cool it. Be cool and nobody will get hurt!"

"Let's go, Tommy, will you? Come on, man!"

Tommy backed toward the door slowly, pointing the gun down at them. "I could shoot you all right now! Kill you all, so don't get ideas. Remember, I'm mad enough to do it, just for kicks . . . shit! So don't move."

As Carlos pulled at the door, two men who were coming in stumbled and fell against it. The door swung open and hit Carlos. The impact caused him to lose his footing, and he was thrown against the counter, bumping into Tommy.

"Watch out. Stickup!" yelled Chiquitín.

Turning, Tommy fired toward Chiquitín. In an instant Tommy and Carlos darted around the two men and headed out into the street.

"Ay . . . ay . . . Dios mío! Por Dios, God, he's been shot! Chiquitín!" Lali's screams filled the luncheonette, echoing outside. Blood poured out of Chiquitín's left shoulder, covering the floor and a large area of Lali's white uniform.

Rudi rushed into the back and grabbed his thirty-eight caliber revolver. "I'll kill those bastards!" As he rushed out, one of the men followed.

"Holdup! Holdup! Help . . ." he yelled, after Rudi. Several shots were heard.

"Chiquitín," Lali screamed. "Help . . . ayuda . . . help us!" She put her arm around him. She looked up at the other man, who was staring at them. "Get an ambulance. . . . Call the police!"

"Right away." The man rushed to the pay phone near the entrance and dialed the police emergency number. "We'll get an ambulance right away, don't worry. He'll be O.K."

"Chiquitín, let me get something to stop the bleeding." Lali looked at Chiquitín, hesitating.

"Go on, Lali; I'm O.K. Go on," Chiquitín said weakly.

Lali got up. "Tell them to send an ambulance right away!" she called to the man on the phone.

"There's been a robbery and someone's been shot!" He spoke loudly into the phone, "Send an ambulance. Yes, it's Rudi's Luncheonette at . . ."

Several people walked into the store, and Lali saw Raquel Martínez.

"Raquel! Por Dios . . . help me here with these towels for Chiquitín; he's been shot!" Quickly they put compresses on the wound on Chiquitín's shoulder to help stop the bleeding.

"Somebody, keep people out . . . it's gonna get crowded in here . . ." Lali spoke to one of the men. "Rick, please . . ."

"All right, everybody," he said, "outside. We gotta keep the door clear for the police and the ambulance."

"Who's been shot in there?" someone asked.

"What can we do to help?"

"Has anybody called the police?"

"We already called the police," said the man who had made the phone call. "Everything's under control. Please stay outside." He and Rick spoke to the crowd, explaining.

"There's been a robbery and a shooting; it's Chiquitín, the dwarf. He's been shot. No, he's not dead, and an ambulance is on the way."

"Where's Rudi?" someone asked.

"Yeah, where is he?"

"Where is Rudi?" Rick called out to Lali.

"Oh!" She remembered that some shots had been fired. "He went after the boys that did it. I better see what's happened." She looked at Chiquitín, who had his eyes closed. "Raquel, please stay . . ."

"Of course."

"Chiquitín," Lali whispered, "the ambulance is coming here any minute. . . . You'll be all right." He nodded weakly.

Lali walked out past the group. They continued to ask questions.

"Lali, where's Rudi?"

"Qué paso?"

"What's happening?"

"Can we help you?"

She ignored their questions and looked down the street. A group of men were standing near the far corner, leading away from the avenue. They stood outside the entrance of a dark narrow alleyway. As she started toward them, she heard sirens. Several police cars stopped in front of the luncheonette, blocking traffic. Lali ran up to them.

"Miss, are you all right . . . are you hurt?" a policeman asked, as he stepped out of the patrol car.

She realized that her white uniform was drenched with blood. "I'm all right. . . . There's been a robbery and a shooting. There's a man hurt in there. . . . Please get an ambulance."

"It's coming. Did they get away?"

Lali began to explain, then pointed to the group near the outside of the alleyway.

"My husband went after them . . . maybe he's been shot!" Lali closed her eyes, feeling faint.

"Go on inside, miss; we'll take care of this."

"No, I'm fine. I have to go to see what happened."

"Sorry, lady; get inside the store. There might be shooting."

"But, please . . . I—"

"No way, lady. Now I don't have time to argue." Quickly he motioned two policemen into the luncheonette. "Shit," he yelled out. "Why the hell didn't somebody cover that end of the street?" Jumping into a patrol car, he signaled for two other cars to follow.

Without hesitating or looking at the policemen who entered the luncheonette, Lali started at a fast run after the patrol cars.

She saw the police stop the cars and head into the alleyway.

One of the men left the group and came running toward her. "Lali, he's got the two boys that held up the store and he's gonna kill them. He won't give up the gun to la policía."

She heard Rudi's voice arguing with the same policemen who had spoken to her.

"Don't do it, mister; you'll be in a lotta trouble for nothing. Just give us the gun; come on, now."

She looked in the alleyway and saw the tall boy, Tommy, slumped down on the ground against the wall, crouching and holding his stomach in pain. It was dark in the alleyway; the street lamp sent in a dim glimmer of light. Tommy's hands glistened, reflecting the wetness of his own blood. His sunglasses had fallen off and he looked even younger than before. Carlos was standing with his back pressed against the wall, staring terrified at Rudi. He held his hands over his head, clutching his green suede cap, and trembled. Rudi stood less than three feet away, pointing his gun at him.

"Please, mister," Carlos sobbed, "don't shoot me. Don't shoot."

"Hijos de la gran puta! Animales, I should shoot you down like dogs . . . scum! You don't wanna work, only steal and harm innocent people. Ladrones, desgraciados! The world would be better off without you!"

"O.K., mister!" The policeman warned, "Give us your gun now. . . . Come on, this is police business. We'll take care of them. You done all you had to . . . Drop it now!"

"Rudi!" Lali shouted. "Please don't . . . don't shoot. They are only kids. Give the policía your gun, por Dios, for God's sakes."

Rudi turned to look at Lali, and for the first time seemed to notice that there were people and police standing beside him.

"Kids? You call these kids? Animals, monsters, that's what they are." He lowered the gun and looked at the policeman. "Here," he said handing over the gun.

Instantly the police went over to the two boys. "Sergeant, we need an ambulance; this kid's bleeding bad."

"Is he gonna die, officer?" Carlos's voice was heard as they led him away. His hands were handcuffed behind his back, and he was still clutching his cap. "Is he gonna die . . . is he?"

"Listen," the sergeant asked Rudi, "did you shoot that kid?" Rudi nodded. "You got a permit for this gun?"

"Yes."

"O.K., now, listen, I gotta take you down to the station and question you to find out what's happened."

"They keep ripping me off . . . and I'm not gonna take it!" Rudi shouted. "You know how many hours a day we work for a few dollars? How many years of sacrifice it took to get somewhere? To buy a small business? I'm not letting no punks rob me."

"All right." The sergeant interrupted. "I understand. Where's your permit, back at the store? O.K., well, I have to have your permit. Sit in back of the car, and we'll go to your store first."

The patrol car backed up to the luncheonette. An ambulance was parked in front.

"How's Chiquitín?" Rudi asked.

"I don't know." Lali shook her head. "I hope it's only the shoulder." She began to cry.

When they got inside, Chiquitín was already on the stretcher, his body covered with a sheet. But he looked up at her and smiled. His half-brothers Paco and Ralphy were with him.

"They're taking him to emergency," Paco said. "I'm going with him, and Ralphy is waiting for Mami to get back. It's a good thing she went shopping and don't have to see this."

"Chiquitín?" Lali took his hand, holding it tightly. "How do you feel? I have to answer some questions, but as soon as I finish, I'll be down to the hospital."

"I'm fine, don't worry. I'll be just fine."

"That was a brave thing to do, warning the customers that way," Rudi said to Chiquitín. "Whatever we can do for you, you know we will."

"All right, mister, where's your permit?" The sergeant looked at Rudi. "You better have one, because that kid you shot might die!"

"It's right here, officer, in my wallet, wait." Rudi found his wallet among the items that he emptied out on the counter.

"O.K." The sergeant turned to call to another police officer. "Dooley, how are you doing with witnesses? Make sure you get as many eyewitnesses as possible. All right! Now . . ." He turned to Rudi.

"Here you are." Rudi handed the sergeant the gun permit.

"O.K."—the sergeant looked it over carefully—"that's in order. You're lucky." He opened a pad and began to write. "Now, before we go down to the station, tell me what happened."

"We were serving our customers as usual, when these two young punks come in . . ." Rudi explained.

The sergeant took notes, interrupting Rudi to ask questions. "Did you actually see them go into the alley?"

"No, but I saw them head in that direction . . . and I said to myself, 'they might just be hiding in there!' Just a hunch, you know? Sure enough, I pass by the alley and they fired a few shots at me. You see they don't know you can't get out of the alleyway. . . . It's a dead-end. So, they were stuck, and I just turned, aimed, and fired."

"And then?"

"That's it . . . I got that punk good, and the other pendejo starts yelling, drops his gun . . . crying at me . . . dirty stinking cowards."

"O.K., now, let me just check out our witnesses. Then you have to go down to the station. You too, miss. We won't keep you, but we have to set things right. We'll finish up and you can come back."

"Can we go to the hospital, officer," Lali asked, "to find out how our friend is?"

"Once we finish at the station, miss, you can go anywhere you like."

PART TWO

"Mira, Wilfredo, is that crazy woman still out there?" Rudi asked a customer as he entered the luncheonette.

"Yeah, she's still out there talking to anybody who'll listen."

"You see that? If she were a man, she wouldn't dare behave that way, you know? Pero, she's a woman, so she knows I can't hit her." Rudi walked over to the front window and looked out. "Coño, she's been out there since early this morning, and she don't stop. This is the third day!"

"Listen, Rudi, why don't you call the police—tell them she's bothering your place of business?" asked Wilfredo.

"Why? Because I already called them! Twice the first day and several times yesterday. You know, they came and spoke to her. They say, Be good, leave this man alone and go home. O.K., that's all. She agrees, goes around the corner and when the police leave, she comes right back, eh? What can I do? I don't wanna keep calling them for that crazy fool!"

"Rudi, is she still out there?" Lali walked in from the back kitchen.

"Yeah, she's out there all right . . . and making a racket right in the street! Take a look!"

"She's making speeches!" Wilfredo said. "She's stopping the whole neighborhood and telling how you killed her son . . . shot him in cold blood and all!"

"You see?" Rudi shook his head, "I defended myself, my family, my business, and I'm a murderer! Her thief of a son shot my helper, Chiquitín, and would have killed us if I let him. He robbed us . . . Carajo! Damn it, that kid of hers was no angel!"

"Well, she don't see it that way." Wilfredo shrugged and walked over to the front window, looking out into the street.

"Look at that? Look! All them people gathering around her . . . listening to her. . . . Look!" Rudi called to Lali.

"Ay, Rudi, please forget her. Nobody's going to listen to her; she's just upset."

"But it's three months since this whole business is over. . . . What's the matter with her? Hasn't she got a family and a home to go to? And why is she bothering me now?"

"Come on." Lali walked over to Rudi. "Let's go on with our work!"

"She's gonna chase the customers away, Lali."

"No, she's not. Our customers are still coming in. Right, Wilfredo?"

"That's right, Rudi," Wilfredo agreed. "She's only a novelty now, you know, something to amuse the neighborhood, but people don't really pay attention to that kind of talk."

"But look . . . see? They are all listening to that crazy woman. What the hell is she saying, anyway?" Rudi opened the door.

"It is fair? What has happened to me, good people, please listen!" They heard a woman's voice speaking in Spanish. "Bendito . . . what he did to my son . . ."

"I'm not taking this abuse without defending myself." Rudi walked out.

"Rudi! Rudi! Don't get involved in that. Come back in," Lali called out after him.

Rudi walked toward the crowd that had gathered around the woman. They all stood in front of the tenement stoop steps adjoining the luncheonette.

"Listen! Listen to me! Tomás Ivan Rodriguez was fifteen. . . . Fifteen years was all that he was allowed to live in this world before he was shot down like a dog and buried without a marker! I am all alone. I cannot have his father make things right." Roberta Rodriguez was a small thin olive-skinned woman, with deep lines in her face, and very thin arms. She spoke passionately and expressively in a shrill voice. "He must have a headstone to show that he was part of this world. Dios mío . . . God in Heaven has to help me reach that man who shot my boy!"

"Mrs. Rodriguez!" Rudi shouted. The people gathered about her stepped back, making room for Rudi. "What are you doing here? Why don't you go home! I was cleared of any charges at the hearing . . . cleared! There is nothing in the record against me. So why don't you accept what your son did and what he was, eh? I defended myself and my wife and my employee. I am not a murderer, Mrs. Rodriguez, but your son was a thief and he shot an innocent person. Your son, who—"

"Oh," interrupted Mrs. Rodriguez, "so you came out at last! It took me three days to get you out! You don't wanna hide no more in your store . . . a respectable businessman that is afraid to talk to a woman alone. Face me, come on! Tell me you didn't shoot my son down like a dog!"

"I was cleared of all charges by the court. Your being here ain't gonna do nothing or accomplish nothing. I acted in self-defense and everyone here knows it!"

"You shot my boy. He was only fifteen years old. He's not coming back to harm you no more. I don't care who cleared you. You have an obligation to my son! You shot a boy, not an animal! You say the courts cleared you, eh? But"—Mrs. Rodriguez pointed up raising her arm—"these good people here know better! What about God? Are you cleared with Him? Listen to this hardhearted man who won't listen to a mother's lament for her dead son!"

"What the hell do you want from me, lady? Your son got just what he deserved! He was a thief with a gun who almost killed my helper, an innocent person!"

"That was an accident. Carlos told me how it happened. Anyway, your helper is alive today. He is living, working, he is with his family, but my son is—"

"Look there, Mrs. Rodriguez!" He pointed to Old Mary. She was standing by the stoop steps watching. "There is my helper's mother. She almost lost a son, and I almost lost my life and maybe even my wife's life, all on account of your wonderful innocent son! And what about that mother, eh? Old Mary? and me? and my wife?"

"You are still alive!" Roberta Rodriguez looked at Old Mary. "Forgive my son, for what he did was wrong. But your son is still alive and you can see him and touch him, eh? Forgive the pain Tommy caused you and yours, but pity me now, as I suffer for any trouble he caused. You understand what I am saying, señora. I can see you do." Old Mary remained silent and lowered her eyes. Mrs. Rodriguez turned to look at Rudi. "She understands . . . but you are a hardhearted man, calling the police on a defenseless woman. You have no conscience!"

Rudi looked around him; more people were gathering, and he saw his neighbors and steady customers looking at him and at Mrs. Rodriguez.

"All right, I'm out here now. What do you want? For God's sakes, why are you here after three months? What do you want from me?" Rudi shouted. "What does this woman want from my life?"

"A headstone!" Roberta Rodriguez's shrill voice sounded over the heads of the crowd. "A headstone, Mr. Padillo, so that everyone may know that my son Tommy once lived, and so I will have a place to go and mourn him, a place with his name and the name of his parents!

Wait here . . ." Excitedly, she held out a sheet of paper. "Here, for three months I have been looking and shopping for a headstone. It explains it all here. How much it costs and when it can be delivered, everything. It costs three hundred dollars. You can see I am here because I have no money, no family, no husband. I have three small children; one of them is disabled. I have no one else to turn to." She walked over to Rudi. "Here . . . see, look for yourself. I have shopped carefully, and here is the most reasonable one."

"Are you crazy?" Rudi stepped away from her. "Why should I give you that kind of money? What is it to me?" He looked around him and shrugged. Everyone was silent.

"But you have an obligation. It was you who killed my son—you are now responsible! I just explained there is no one else."

"Are you outta your mind? Get away!"

"You, yes, you! If you had let Tommy live, things would be different. But you went after him and you caught him and now he's gone. You must help me. I have no one else to turn to."

"Oh, no, lady! No, sir! This is nothing to me." Rudi turned, walking away. "This woman is stark raving nuts."

"Wait, wait! Mr. Padillo!" Mrs. Rodriguez held on to Rudi's arm, thrusting the sheet of paper in front of him. "Here, look at this, please, just look at it."

"You are crazy, let go of me!" Rudi pulled his arm away. "Three hundred dollars for a headstone! A headstone? I never heard of such a thing. Listen to me, Mrs. Rodriguez. I'll call the police if you don't leave and stop making such a nuisance of yourself."

"Go ahead. I won't go away! I'll come here every day!"

"They'll put you away for being a lunatic. You— you—" Rudi hesitated. "What about your children? Go home to them; take care of your children. Get out of here!"

"I'll come here every day! I'll mourn for Tommy right here in front of your store! For the rest of my life, if I have to!"

"Mourn your thieving no-good son here, or anyplace else you want, but you ain't getting one penny from me!"

She watched as Rudi walked quickly back into the luncheonette, slamming the door behind him. Turning, she looked about the crowd as they watched her.

"Listen, you all know that I'm right, eh? I'm only asking for justice!" She caught Old Mary's eye and called out to her, "Señora, your son, how is he?" Old Mary started to walk into her building. "Please, señora, is your son all right now?" Old Mary nodded. "Good. You have my sympathy as a mother. What my boy Tommy did was wrong. But your son is alive and I am happy for you. Tell me, please, can you help me reach this man?" Old Mary turned away and disappeared into the building. "It's all right, then, I understand. But still, my son must have a headstone on his grave, something to show he was alive once and . . ." Slowly people began to disperse. "Wait. Where are you all going? Listen to me! Why do we have to kill each other this way? Why do we have to shoot our own? Por Dios . . . God in heaven. Virgen María . . . I know now how you suffered for your son. We shoot our own . . . we crucify our own." Except for a few young people, off to the side, everyone had left. "Go on, go ahead, all of you! Leave! Go on! But I'm staying right here and I'm mourning my boy! You! You!" she called out to a young boy in the small group of youngsters. "Mira, how old are you, son?"

"Thirteen and a half." He smiled. Two of the girls giggled nervously.

"What's your name?" The boy answered in a low voice. "What's that? I can't hear you. What's your name, son?" A girl giggled loudly, and a boy smacked him on the back.

"Tuto. They call me Tuto."

"Tuto! Don't do nothing bad, nothing wrong to hurt your mama, you hear? See how I'm suffering for my boy? Don't do nothing bad. Stay away from bad friends." The small group of youngsters began to giggle. "Tuto, you promise me that? Yes?"

"Yes." Tuto nodded.

"She's nuts, man." Another boy whispered, "Daffy."

"Yeah, está loca," a girl agreed.

As Roberta Rodriguez started toward them, the small group of youngsters backed away.

"Be careful she don't get you, Tuto!" one of the boys teased, pushing Tuto toward her.

"Get outta here, stupid." Tuto went after the boy.

"Bendito, don't be scared. I'm not crazy like they say. Wait a minute." The young people continued to back away. "O.K." She stopped. "Agh, go ahead, leave—all of you! I'm staying right here, and I'm mourning my boy." Looking around her, she started to lament in sing-song. "Tommy, I won't desert you. Tommy, you will have a headstone with your name . . . with our names. Tomás Ivan Rodriguez born to Felipe Ignacio Rodriguez and Roberta Rodriguez fifteen years ago! A baby boy! Tommy, I won't desert you!" She walked back and forth in front of the luncheonette and tenement entrance, chanting her lament.

"Look at that!" Rudi looked out of the front store window. "She won't stop. Hasn't she got somebody to take her home and put some sense in her head?" He shook his head with disgust.

Several men sat at the counter.

"I'll tell you one thing," one of the men said, "she seems pretty determined to me."

"And I'll tell you another thing." Rudi snapped, "So am I—determined she ain't getting one cent from me! You know how much that dead punk cost me? In time and aggravation? And I had to do right by Chiquitín when he was in the hospital, eh? Three weeks it took for him to recover from that gunshot . . . and all that time I gave Old Mary his salary, without fail! Not that I minded that. After all, it was a brave thing he did, warning my customers. And thank God he's back to work and everything's all right again. But, well, this has not been an easy time for me either . . . and she gets nothing from me. Nevermind!"

"Rudi, maybe we should try to talk to her," Lali said, "explain to her that we cannot give her money for what she wants."

"Talk to her? She's nuts just to ask for such a thing. You cannot reason with that kind of person. Look, I'm telling the police that I'll do what's necessary to swear out a warrant for her arrest, if she keeps this up!"

"O.K., but before we do that, let's talk—"

"No!" interrupted Rudi, shouting. "No. And I don't want you, Lali, to be talking to no crazy woman, you hear? I don't give one penny for that dead louse! Even if I have to get a lawyer. I'll spend the money like that, and that's all!"

Lali looked at her husband and said nothing, returning to her work. Customers spoke in low voices among themselves. Rudi continued to look out the window as he worked, making gestures of annoyance and commenting on the way Mrs. Rodriguez marched up and down in front of the store.

For almost two weeks Roberta Rodriguez had continued her vigil for her dead son. She would walk back and forth in front of Rudi's Luncheonette, chant, and sway from side to side. She would do this until closing time, which was about eleven at night.

Rudi and Lali had gone down to the police station to find out if Mrs. Rodriguez had any family who could per-

suade her to go home. The police were able to tell them
that she had only one adult living relative in New York,
a cousin who did not want to become involved. If she had
relatives who could be responsible for her, they were all
in Puerto Rico; as far as they knew, no one was here.

The police were tired of coming to take Mrs. Rodriguez
away and were annoyed at Rudi and his constant phone
calls. "Can't you take care of this yourself, Mr. Padillo?
She's perfectly harmless." The police officer had spoken
curtly and was irritable with Rudi; so the next week
Rudi made plans to swear out a warrant for Mrs. Rodriguez's arrest.

"Now they will have to put that crazy woman in jail!"
he had said.

That week she spent very little time at her vigil. She
did not appear at all on Wednesday. A customer com-
plained in jest to Rudi the next day.

"Bueno, Rudi, it's just not the same around here today.
Look at the time, it's almost five o'clock and Mrs. Rodriguez is missing."

By now everyone in the neighborhood had become used
to her and most of the time no one paid her any mind.

"Thank God!" Rudi responded. "Soon it will be cold
again and she won't be able to stay out there all day and
night making a nuisance of herself. I pray for an early
winter. She should be missing permanently!"

"Wait . . . talk of the devil! Here she comes." A man
seated near the window pointed out into the street.

"Ay, and I thought we would have another peaceful

day!" Rudi said annoyed. "Tsk . . . bendito!" Looking out into the street, he saw that Mrs. Rodriguez was coming into the store. "Wait a minute—is she coming in here? I don't believe this."

There were only a half dozen customers in the small luncheonette: four men and two women. They all turned to look at the entrance, waiting for the door to open.

"I'm gonna throw her out bodily, that's what I'm gonna do!" Rudi squared his shoulders and called out, "Lali! Lali! Look who's coming to make more trouble."

Lali stopped working in the back kitchen and came out front. The door opened, and Mrs. Rodriguez held up her right hand, with an open palm, and entered.

"Peace, good friends, please, peace! Hear me out. I have—"

"Get outta here." Rudi walked quickly from behind the counter and faced her. "Out! Do you hear? Right now! Go on!"

"Wait, I have not come to make trouble." Still holding up an open palm, she gestured toward Rudi. "Peace, I said. Don't abuse me, please, Mr. Padillo."

"Ha! Abuse you? It is you who are abusing us. You come into my place of business, you disturb my customers—"

"Sir, your customers are also your neighbors and are also human. They understand. Isn't that so?" She looked at those watching her. "Let me say what I have to say and then I go! I have come here for the last time today."

"Listen to me, Mrs. Rodriguez, if you have something

to say, say it fast! I am swearing out a warrant for your arrest. You ain't gonna get away with this nonsense no longer. So, you better behave and then leave. I don't want to put you in jail, but I will!"

"Only a few words and then I will go . . . and I won't come back here. You have to know the facts about things, Mr. Padillo, and there must be witnesses." Roberta Rodriguez nodded and looked around her. "You, too, miss"— she nodded at Lali—"all must listen. It seems I must not come here again or I will be arrested. It seems that if I keep my oldest daughter out of school so that she may care for my disabled boy, while I am doing a mother's duty—the duty of seeking justice for my dead son—they will take my children away from me. Yes, here in this country—they will take my children away! Because they know what's best for them. Strangers know what's best for me and my children. A mother here is not worth much, eh? A family is torn apart . . . and I can do nothing . . . but, no matter! I have done my best; I have tried with all my heart and strength to have justice done. This will be my final plea."

Mrs. Rodriguez hesitated and looked directly at Rudi, speaking in a piercing pitch, "A headstone! You owe me and my son and my family a headstone, sir! When you decided to take my boy's life, did you think he was alone? Did you consider me, and his brother and sisters? Did you consider that he would be gone from us forever? His grave must be marked with something permanent! Now there is a piece of shrubbery, nothing else, on his grave.

In time I will not be able to tell it from any other grave! Right now I have trouble finding him when I go there. You must help us. You must see that my boy rests in peace with a permanent headstone telling us where he is . . . and who he was. I don't want to lose him in death too."

"Are you finished?" Rudi pointed to the door. "Because, if that's all, lady, please leave!"

"But"—Roberta Rodriguez held out a sheet of paper— "take this please and reconsider your answer to me. Surely three hundred dollars is not so much compared to a boy's life? I haven't got the money. I can hardly feed my children as it is. I'm on public assistance . . . don't you see? I have no one else. Here, take this and look. I shopped carefully. There are low cost payment terms—either weekly or by the month. Believe me, I spent a lot of time shopping before I—"

"Get out of here! Get out before I throw you out!"

"Just take this sheet of paper and I'll leave . . . please. Mr. Padillo, don't make me beg. I don't like to beg, but for my children I'll beg. For me, it doesn't matter. Bury me anywhere. I don't even want a grave . . . but please take this. I promise you before Jesus Christ and all that's holy, and these good people here are my witnesses, that if you take this piece of paper and read it, I will not bother you again! Ever! I promise, please—"

"Caramba!" Rudi closed his eyes. "I don't believe this woman! Will you leave?"

"Please, here." She held out the sheet of paper. "Take it."

The store was silent. Everyone watched as she thrust the paper in front of Rudi. Rudi sighed, opening his mouth to protest, but said nothing.

He reached for the piece of paper, "Gimme. Now get out and don't ever come back!"

"Thank you." Mrs. Rodriguez smiled. "The Lord will make you reconsider. He's heard my prayers. My dead son and my family will forgive you . . . and God will bless you." Swiftly she left.

Rudi stood perfectly still, holding the sheet of paper. "This whole business is crazy. What the hell does she think my taking this piece of paper is gonna do for her?"

"Ain't you gonna read it, Rudi?" a woman asked.

"Yeah," a man said, "ain't you curious?"

Turning, he looked at his customers and held up the sheet of paper, tearing it in two, then in four, then into tiny little bits.

"There, that's what I'm gonna do with it!" He went back around the counter, tossing the scraps of paper into the trash. "Good riddance."

"Poor woman," said Lali.

"How can you say poor woman, after the way she drove us nuts?"

"She's very upset, that's why," Lali replied.

"Hey, Rudi, maybe you should've read the paper," another woman said. "Who knows, maybe you could change your mind."

"No." Rudi shook his head emphatically. "I could never change my mind."

"Well, one never knows for sure. You might have." The man by the window looked around and winked.

"Yeah, Rudi," another man said, with good humor, "you could have been persuaded—how can you tell? Now you will never know!"

"That's right," Rudi responded. "Now none of us will ever know!" Turning to Lali, he called out, "Lali, tonight on the blue plate special, let's add a dessert."

Coming to Terms

Old Mary stood outside on the stoop steps of her building, holding the old plastic carseat cushion and a can of beer. She placed the cushion on a clean spot near the railing, and sat down. She had cooked the evening meal, served everyone, cleaned her kitchen; now, while it was still daylight and warm, she sat enjoying the outdoors. Old Mary sipped beer and greeted her neighbors as they passed by. Most commented on the weather.

"Who would believe it's now the end of October," a man spoke to Old Mary as he passed by. "The radio said it went up to eighty-eight degrees today! Imagine? Caramba . . . and only Monday it was so cold I had to wear my coat!"

"What a crazy country, eh?" Old Mary responded and waved as he walked on.

She looked with amusement at a group of boys carrying baseball equipment. They were laughing, shouting, and pushing each other as they hurried toward the schoolyard. Two little girls took turns hopping on one leg and bouncing a Spaulding ball on the area they had chalked out for their street game.

In a short while, the little girls left and the street got quieter. It was cooler as nightfall set in.

"Mami . . . " Old Mary looked over to see her son Chiquitín standing next to her. "I'm going to work. Is there anything you want before I go?"

"No, mi hijo, everything's fine."

"Bendición, Mami." Chiquitín waited.

"God bless you, son." She watched as he went next door and entered the luncheonette.

The streetlights cast long shadows as people walked by; an occasional car horn was heard. Old Mary heard thunder, and in the distance, over the rooftops, she saw a flash of lightning illuminate the sky. A light rain began to fall. Old Mary stood, stretched, and picked up the plastic cushion. She stepped up to the entrance of her building, glancing once more at the street. The rain was beginning to come down with force; the stoop, the sidewalk, and the street were now covered with a layer of water, giving the surface a brilliance. Good, it'll get a good washing around here. Old Mary inhaled, smelling the freshness of the rain.

Just before turning to go inside, she saw Rudi rushing toward the pile of garbage out on the curb. He vigorously stuffed some trash into a large overcrowded garbage can. He started back, then stopped abruptly. She watched as he placed his hands on his hips and began speaking to someone.

"What the hell? I don't believe this! Didn't I tell you I was gonna shoot you if I caught you around here again? Didn't I warn you?"

Old Mary leaned out from under the protection of the entrance and held the cushion over her head to keep the rain away from her. She squinted, trying to see better.

"And for a long time you didn't dare come here, eh? But now you think you can start your nonsense again!"

Old Mary saw the old orange cat, who sat a few feet away, looking up almost defiantly at Rudi.

"You old bastard, you! What do you want?" The cat took a couple of steps toward Rudi, then stopped at a safe distance. It meowed several times, looking at him. "You miserable thing you . . . you must've been in a bad fight this time! Look at you, you mangy old thing, all wet and messed up. They almost killed you! But you're still looking for trouble, coming around here, you know that?" Rudi paused and they eyed each other silently for a moment. Then the cat emitted one long piercing yowl.

"O.K., está bien . . . I'm gonna fix you. You wanna take a chance with me, eh? We gonna come to terms, you and me! Just wait, I'll fix you."

Old Mary watched as Rudi ran into the store. She looked at the cat, which didn't move. It sat in the same spot, drenched, looking in Rudi's direction, waiting.

"You still here?" Rudi walked toward the cat. "Come on, you old son of a bitch! You won! You know, you won!" He carried an old saucer full of milk. "I ain't gonna shoot you. Here!" Rudi put the saucer of milk down a few feet away from the cat and waited. The cat blinked at him but did not move. "Goddamn." Rudi chuckled. "I can't shoot you. . . . We come to terms already, eh? Anybody who lasts as long as you don't die so easy!" Laughing, Rudi hurried out of the rain into the luncheonette.

Old Mary saw the cat cautiously approach the saucer of milk and begin lapping it up hungrily. She smiled, and shook her head, then disappeared inside her building.

The cat finished the milk, and slowly, with some effort, it walked over to the alleyway near the far corner of the block. There it found a dry spot on a piece of corrugated cardboard that had been placed on the sill of a cellar window. A few times its sleep was disturbed by a speeding car or someone's footsteps passing by; but for the most part, the night remained quiet, and the cat slept peacefully.

Nicholasa Mohr a native of Manhattan's El Barrio, is the author of numerous short stories, essays and books for children, young adults and adults. Her books include *Nilda*, *El Bronx Remembered*, *Felita*, *Going Home*, *In Nueva York*, *Rituals of Survival: A Woman's Portfolio*, and most recent, *Growing Up Inside the Sanctuary of My Imagination*, *In My Own Words*. From 1988 through 1991, she was the distinguished visiting professor at Queens College of CUNY. Some of the prestigious awards she has been honored with are: an honorary degree of Doctor of Letters from the State University of New York in 1989, Albany Campus, the American Book Award in 1981 and a National Book Award Finalist in 1976. Her works have been translated into Spanish and Japanese.

Her forthcoming works include *The Song of El Coquí*, and *Tales of Puerto Rico*, (Viking Penguin, 1995); *The Magic Shell*, (Scholastic, 1995); *Old Letivia and the Mountain of Sorrows*, (Viking Penguin, 1996).